SAY
YES

SAY
YES

AUDREY COULOUMBIS

G. P. PUTNAM'S SONS / NEW YORK

ACKNOWLEDGMENTS

Never, in my wildest dreams, could I have imagined this book would enjoy the benefit of such intense and unwavering effort and fierce support from so many people whose names should appear on the title page along with mine.

I want to thank the year 2000 Newbery committee members for their vote of confidence in my future as a writer.

And I want to thank my husband, my writer's group, my agent, my editor and her many associates, and my publisher for generous, enthusiastic, and encouraging feedback when the challenges of this book proved daunting. And finally, we all appreciate the comments of one of my favorite librarians who, in the eleventh hour, put us all back on the right track. Thank you, Kate McClelland.

Library of Congress Cataloging-in-Publication Data
Couloumbis, Audrey. Say yes / Audrey Couloumbis.
p. cm. Summary: In her efforts to hang on following the disappearance of her stepmother, Casey resorts to anything, including robbery. [1. Stepmothers—Fiction. 2. Missing persons—Fiction. 3. Stealing—Fiction.] I. Title.
PZ7.C8305 Say 2002 [Fic]—dc21 2001048126
ISBN 0-399-23390-3 10 9 8 7 6 5 4 3 2 1 First Impression

For Aunt Adrienne, who shared her story

ONE

Wednesday morning is likc any other but different.

I eat cereal from a box, brush my teeth and get dressed. That's the part that's like any other morning.

My stepmother, Sylvia, gets up. Before eight. To see me off to school, she says. That's the different part.

She comes into the kitchen just as I finish eating. Her mascara's rubbed off, leaving dark rings under her eyes. She picks up my lunch bag and asks, "You made peanut butter and jelly?"

"I can always trade it," I say, rinsing out the cereal bowl.

"My mistake," she says, rolling her eyes. "I thought the idea was to take what you want in the first place." She looks into the fridge as if she expects to find another lunch waiting.

I pull on my jacket. "I don't have time to mess around."

She makes a faint annoyed sound with her tongue. Shuts the fridge door, sets the bag down on the counter like it's a problem she's about to solve. Opens the bread box. "Did we have any of those chocolate things you like so much?"

"Nope."

"I'll try to pick some up today, okay?" she asks.

The phone rings.

I'm closest, I pick up. It's him. The boyfriend. He clears his throat before he asks, "Is this Cassandra?" and I say, "No," because that isn't my name. Then I let the receiver clatter on the counter.

Sylvia reaches for it, not even giving me the you-could-be-nice look. The guy she's dating, Jim, wears too much cologne, the kind that smells like roach poison. He chews Certs all the time, except when he's chewing ice cubes. Sylvia says the Certs are because he's in a business where it's important his smile is fresh. I don't trust his smile. He's always smiling when he treats me like a turnstile, a thing he has to go through to get to Sylvia. He doesn't know I'm a person.

She tells him, "Just give me ten minutes. I'll call you back."

She tries to brush wisps of hair back from my forehead as she hangs up. She's always playing with my hair, clutching at me, something. I grab my lunch and pull away to get my books.

"You're a good girl, do you know that, Casey?"

"Good enough." Sylvia follows me to the door, sort of clinging to me with invisible strings.

I used to like the feeling this gives me, like she can't quite bring herself to let go. I still like it, I just don't like that I like it. I'm twelve, too old for kid stuff. She watches me all the way to the elevator. I'm pretending I don't know she's there. Strings.

When I glance back, her hair is sticking up like the ears on a little white dog. Her eyes look huge and dark. Sometimes a glimpse of her goes right to my heart, the way this one does. She's more than a person can take in the morning.

"You look like a raccoon," I say as the elevator door opens.

The building superintendent, Mr. Loach, is in the elevator along with his kid, Paulie, who is maybe fifteen. They always look like they've been cleaning up in the boiler room or something.

Paulie looks at me like he's about to say hi, but then Mr. Loach says, "You're Sylvie's kid, ain't you?"

I nod.

"Cute, that Sylvie," Mr. Loach says. "I like her."

I look away. One thing Sylvia always tells me, don't worry about being rude to grown-ups if you think they might not be very nice. Mr. Loach strikes me as not very nice.

TWO

When I get home from school, Sylvia isn't in the kitchen, the way she sometimes is, holding a cup of coffee in both hands. Staring out the window at this little patch of blue sky. Her patch.

A few minutes later, I notice the lamp is on in the living room. Sylvia does that when she's gone to work before I get home. So maybe someone called in sick and she had to go in. I told her I'm too old for this kind of thing. But I leave the lamp on anyway.

Around seven-thirty, I get kind of uneasy. My homework isn't done. I've been sitting in front of the television eating junk food. Plus there's money in an envelope under a magnet on the fridge. Five tens and a five. It isn't like Sylvia to leave money around.

She should get home a little after nine. So I spread my books and notebook out on the dining room table to study, keeping the TV remote next to me. At nine-fifteen, she hasn't come home.

At nine-thirty, she is officially late. Probably out with him.

I stay up a while longer. Listening. A bus stops at the corner, the bus with the squeaky brake. The elevator is next to our apartment, right next to my bedroom wall. It makes a knocking sound when it's going to stop.

Then there are noises in the apartment, stuff I never notice when Sylvia is home. Creepy. Maybe I'll put the chain on, it would serve her right.

Finally, at twelve-fifteen, I get into bed, leaving the light on in the living room. It takes a long time to fall asleep.

THREE

In the morning, the lamp is still on in the living room. Sylvia's funny that way, sometimes she needs a light to go to sleep.

I sock-skate by her room. I like having the apartment to myself in the morning. When I leave for school, it's still kind of dark. I leave the lamp on.

It's a long walk and cold. Paper trash blowing all over the place.

Paulie is across the street from the high school with a bunch of other kids. I used to think he was a lost prince, like in some fairy tale Sylvia read. That he was being hidden with the Loaches until it was time to come back and be king.

That's the kind of stuff I used to think up when I was little. Weird. When the other kids break away from him, Paulie gets into an old blue car.

I get to class late, and my so-called friend, Karen, acts like I'm invisible. Karen is like that, touchy. I ignore her right back. Then, after class, she says, "I thought you were going to call last night," and I say, "I forgot."

"You forgot?" She's ticked off.

"Sylvia had stuff we had to do." I get ticked off, too. Karen could be nice.

The bell rings and kids turn around in their seats, settling down. While Mrs. Zeller is checking attendance, I get to thinking. I would have called Karen except that I got distracted, eating all the cookies and stuff, and watching TV. And waiting for Sylvia.

The one good thing about Karen is, she calls when she says she will.

I scribble *I'm sorry* on a scrap of paper. Leonard, the nerdy kid who sits between us, reads the note before he passes it across to Karen. She looks at it, crumples it into a tight little wad, and flicks it back at me, like a spitball.

It hits Leonard. And bounces away.

Around second period I'm wishing I'd looked in Sylvia's room. Maybe she came home sick. I keep having this thought, suppose she never came home at all. People get murdered all the time. Or robbed and beaten up and left somewhere until someone finds them. I'm practically all Sylvia has in the world, that's what she says.

I hate when she says that.

FOUR

Last week Sylvia asked me to give him another chance. We were shopping. She put strawberry ice cream in the cart. I took it out and put in chocolate mint. Sylvia didn't move on. She waited for an answer.

I said, "It won't do any good. He doesn't like me any better than I like him."

"Maybe he doesn't like you because you didn't like him first," she said. "You didn't like Anthony, either."

"Anthony was okay." At first.

"You didn't think so until I met Salvadore."

"Salvadore was a jerk."

"Agreed," she said. "All I'm saying is, you could be nice. Jim might find out what a sweet kid you really are." Sylvia pulled my coat sleeve. Trying to be cute. Wanting me to say yes.

I know what she likes about him. He buys her stuff. That doesn't change the way he looks at her when she doesn't do things his way. His eyes, like chips of ice. "Maybe the next one will like me first and then I'll like him."

"I want you to like Jim."

"I already don't like him." There was this feeling in the air between us, like the snap in a rubber band.

"Have you ever heard that saying," Sylvia asked me, " 'between a rock and a hard place'? My mother is the rock and you are the hard place."

So we didn't talk about him anymore. We didn't talk much at all.

Leaving the store, she dodged a guy with a briefcase. Then, walking faster and faster to keep up, she never took her eyes off of him. His gray hair curled a little where it touched the collar of his coat, like he needed a haircut.

"It's the other way," I said as she turned a corner. It was late and the wind was pushing at our backs.

Sylvia has no sense of direction. On her way somewhere, she can do a quick run into a store, and when she comes out, she goes back the way she was coming from. I used to ask her, Are we lost? And she would always answer, We know exactly where we are, we just aren't where we planned to be.

"Casey?" She said my name in this high-pitched voice that wasn't like her own at all. It was like hearing the good fairy speaking or something. "Casey?"

"It's not him," I told her. But first I had to step down on this weird sudden hope that sprang up in my own heart. I hated when Sylvia did that to me.

"No," Sylvia said. "You're right."

She thinks she's seeing Dad. Well. Just for a second. My dad died two years ago.

The first time she ever did this, she'd made me run a block

and a half through Fort Tryon Park until we caught up with this guy we didn't know, Sylvia calling, "Harvey! Harvey!" all the way. He'd turned, but not because he heard his name. He turned because he'd heard Sylvia getting closer, just like everybody else we'd passed.

Sylvia stopped when she saw it wasn't Dad. The guy walked just like Dad, Sylvia said. She'd sort of collapsed onto a bench. "Oh, I'm sorry, Casey. I'm just so sorry."

"About what?"

"Well, about this." She'd tried to laugh, which was much better than when she cried. "Making you chase some strange man. Anyone in their right mind knows it can't be him. I must be crazy."

"No, you're not," I said. "You just miss him."

Which was true, and I knew it. But she kept seeing Dad, and I started blaming her when it wasn't him.

FIVE

The lamp is off when I get home from school, that's what I notice first. "Sylvia?" She doesn't answer. "Sylvia?"

Her bed is a mess. The mess looks the same to me as the day before. There are no signs that she made coffee or had anything to eat. My cereal bowl is in the sink. The money is still on the refrigerator door. After a moment of staring at it, I go back to the living room.

I switch the lamp on. Nothing.

I turn the switch a couple of times. On and off.

Nothing.

The bulb's burned out.

S I X

Feeling like I got punched in the stomach, I sit down. Try to figure out what to do. Call the police. Except on TV, a person has to be missing for three days before the police will look for him.

Besides, Sylvia's probably at work. I'm getting myself upset over nothing. I'll walk down to Rocco's Coffee Grill, where she works.

There's sleet coming down, tapping on the windows. It's getting dark. I pull on the long underwear I told her I would never wear and a hat with earflaps that I hate. Wrap my scarf around my neck twice the way she likes me to do.

The cold is terrible. The streets are slippery. On the way, I pass this window that is the sunroom for two parakeets in a big cage. Sylvia and I stop there sometimes and make bird noises at them, and admire their colors. Tonight, the cage isn't at the window. The curtains are drawn shut.

The walk seems to take so long. Three times I almost turn back. I keep going because I can picture finding Sylvia there at the cash register, talking to one of the customers. Telling them how she thinks the bluebird of happiness is really a cheerful yellow. That's the kind of thing Sylvia thinks about when her feet don't hurt.

I have this other picture, like a movie, where she left work in the dark and came down the street and some guy grabbed her purse and knocked her down and she lay there in the street until somebody found her and they took her to the hospital, where she woke up with amnesia and nobody knows who she is.

The wind makes my eyes tear so bad, I have to wipe my face until it hurts. And then I get to Rocco's. Coming in from the cold is so good. The air is warm and smells of garlic bread and roasted meat. Rocco's behind the register, where Sylvia usually is. He's on the phone, putting one hand over the receiver. "Hey, Case. I thought you was gone already."

My ears are so cold, maybe I heard him wrong.

"Hey, let me buy you one last drink," he says.

I nod, looking around for Sylvia.

"You got a cold?" he asks, which makes me think I must look pretty stupid all bundled up.

"Sylvia said I might have a touch of something," I say, stuffing the hat in my pocket. Yanking the scarf loose to hang over my shoulders. "Is she here?"

"Not since she collected her paycheck. She's wound tighter than this telephone cord, ain't she? The guy must be somebody special."

"Sylvia thinks so," I mutter under my breath.

"Well, I think now she gets to call him the fee-an-say," Rocco says. "And you get to call him Daddy."

It takes a moment for the words to sink in. A weak feeling

hits me in the knees. I slide onto one of the stools at the counter. Louella is setting up the coffeemakers for the dinner hour.

"Hey, kiddo." She never remembers my name. Louella never remembers anybody's name.

Rocco hangs up and comes over, perches on the stool next to me.

"Lou," he says. He does some little movement with his fingers to let her know she should give me a soda. "Hey, Case, honey, I didn't mean no disrespect to your real daddy. I just meant—well, it was a stupid thing to say."

"It's okay, Rocco." Everything is so not okay, I don't know what else to say.

"It'll be a big change for you," he says. "It's sudden, I know."

"Yes, it's sudden," I agree.

"Look at it this way," Rocco says. "He's gonna take good care of you and Sylvia. She'll never have to worry about another thing."

"Yeah, that'll help." I sip the soda Louella brings me.

"It's a load off my mind," Rocco says. "I thought Syl would take it really hard, that I sold the place."

"This place? You sold your restaurant?"

"Syl didn't tell you?"

"No."

He shrugs. "Things were coming along well with this guy and all. Probably she didn't want you to worry."

It's all too much to take in at once. "Sylvia lost her job?"

"Somebody wants to put up a big apartment building on this block. It's not a problem, the way things worked out," Rocco says. "I had it in my head already that I want to move south."

I want to ask a lot of questions. All of them back up behind the big one, where's Sylvia? Only Rocco doesn't know.

"Two more days, I turn the key in the lock and I'm outta here." When I don't say anything, Rocco adds, "Now, don't you go getting worried."

"I'm not worried."

"Can I get you something to eat?" Rocco asks. "Sylvia's probably been too busy packing to think about cooking."

"No, thanks." I slip off the stool. "I've got to be going."

"Just came by to say so long, huh?"

"Something like that."

SEVEN

Going back the way I came, the sleet is turning to rain. The wind is in my face. I am cold and trembling and lonelier and unhappier than I have ever been. I wrap the scarf tighter, and for once, I'm glad to have it.

My thoughts are on Sylvia, hoping she's at home.

She might have been out looking for another job. She could right this minute be wondering where I am. I imagine going upstairs and finding the TV on, the burned-out bulb replaced, and in the kitchen, there are Sylvia sounds. The clatter of plates. The *ding!* from the microwave. The whispered swear word when Sylvia burns her fingers opening up dinner.

I'm in a big hurry to get home, taking the shortcut through an empty playground in the dark. By the time I reach my building, I'm running, and I can see our kitchen window.

It's dark.

EIGHT

I flick on the overhead light. Everything is just as I left it.

I check the front of the fridge, scan the kitchen counter, looking for a note.

The freezer is loaded. There are six dinners, all my favorites. None of Sylvia's. "Not a good sign." My voice sounds tough, much tougher than I feel. Almost strong. I shut the freezer.

Six dinners for six days, if I make sandwiches for lunch. Unless I count two frozen dinners a day for Saturday and Sunday. Maybe Sylvia means to be back on the weekend. I go straight through to her bedroom, throw open the closet door.

Mostly everything is gone. She's moved out.

It takes my breath away. There are a few things heaped on the floor. That blue dress she says makes her look fat is still here.

I say, "You are fat."

A terrible anger comes up into my throat. I need to talk to Sylvia.

The boyfriend's number is in Sylvia's book. Jim Neuland. I punch in the numbers, counting on Sylvia to pick up the phone. If he answers, I'll just hang up.

The phone rings twice, then an operator's voice says, "This number has been disconnected. No further informa—"

I slam the receiver down.

She's gone.

I sit by the phone, numb, not even thinking.

Listening to the elevator open and close, to footsteps.

To keys jingling as they're pulled from pockets and handbags. People are coming home from work, turning on the evening news. Cooking dinner. Feeling good about being home where it's warm.

Her mother's number is here. I've called Fran exactly three times in my whole life. All of them during the first week after Sylvia got the job at Rocco's. Sylvia was afraid to let me call her at work.

The first time, I'd smoked up the kitchen by burning the toast. Fran said, "Open the window."

And then Sylvia gave me twenty dollars to pay the electric bill at the convenience store and I lost the money. Fran said, "I'm putting twenty dollars in an envelope and mailing it to you this afternoon. Pay the bill and tell Sylvia she owes her mother lunch."

"Thanks, Fran."

"Don't be so serious. It isn't the end of the world."

And again when I cut my finger. Bad.

Fran asked where on the finger, and how much was it bleeding? She stayed on the phone while I put a Band-Aid on it. "Has the bleeding stopped?" she asked.

"Yes, but it hurts."

"Of course it hurts," Fran said. "Now here's what you do next."

She told me to take a spoonful of whiskey to kill the germs. The bottle was too big to hold with one hand. Fran had instructions for that, too. "Get a juice glass and pour a little in the bottom."

I did. At first, my finger was throbbing. But as I collected the whiskey, the juice glass, and a spoon, and let some whiskey slosh into the glass, I forgot about how much my finger hurt. "Okay," I said when I got back to the phone.

"Now dip the soupspoon in and swallow just the one spoonful."

"Is this going to taste bad?" The stuff smelled terrible.

"Of course. It wouldn't be medicine if it didn't."

So I was prepared for how bad it would taste but not for how it burned going down. I choked and sneezed and picked up the phone again. "Okay."

"So," Fran said. "What were you cutting?"

"The plastic package around the cheese."

"You're hungry?"

"Not anymore."

"Eat cookies or something until Sylvia gets home. And next time, use the scissors."

"I will."

"I have one more thing to recommend."

"What's that?"

"Watch television until Sylvia comes home. It's good to rest after an accident."

"What should I do with the whiskey in the glass?"

"Leave it for Sylvia. Now you're going straight to the television, right?"

"Yes."

"Okay then, you can hang up."

Right after that, Fran and Sylvia'd had a huge fight. Mostly about the wrong way Sylvia did things. That she slept late and didn't try to find a day job so she could be home in the evening, that kind of thing. Sylvia cried when Fran went home.

Worse, they didn't talk for weeks. I can't call Fran. Sylvia would never forgive me for telling her mother on her.

I've been hearing something for a few minutes without really noticing. *Thump, thump, thump, thump, thump.* It's not the elevator. This neighbor, on our other side, turns on his stereo first thing when he gets home. Time to eat.

I get up to put a frozen dinner in the microwave.

I can call Karen. Just to have someone to talk to while I eat. I'm still planning to call her as I turn up the TV.

Like it's a message to me, the news guy tells how this woman left her kids alone in the apartment and got arrested for reckless danger or something. One of the kids isn't even little. Sylvia could be put in jail for going off like this.

I'm glad I haven't told anybody. I can't go to school without brushing my hair anymore. I have to make sure my clothes look nice. Keep everyone from finding out. Not just Fran. And when Sylvia gets back, she'll be proud of me. Grateful, even.

If she comes back.

NINE

At school, I act like there's nothing wrong. During last period, I write to Karen and fold the note into a square so small, the paper won't bend any more. It reads, "Want to come over after school?"

She writes back, "What's Sylvia making for dinner?"

The hair stands on my arms. Like when I realized the light bulb burned out. It's what I should have expected, though. Karen loves Sylvia's cooking.

Sylvia claims she doesn't cook, she just opens boxes and cans. Like this thing she calls a frittata. Frozen hash-brown potatoes and frozen corn and frozen squash, all defrosted and thrown into a big black frying pan with Egg Beaters and shredded cheese. She just pops it into the oven. Even the cheese comes in a package, already shredded. The funny thing is, everything she cooks comes out really good.

There's no need to send an answer back to Karen. It's only ten minutes to the final bell anyway. She comes to my desk as I'm gathering up my stuff.

"Sylvia might not be there," I say. "She has to work late. She left money for us to call out for pizza."

"Cool."

Karen and I like to pretend we're roommates and talk about our jobs and all. Tonight it feels like much more than a game.

Getting on the phone, she tells the pizza guy we're having our boyfriends over, so could he send an extra-large pie. She orders extra toppings without asking if it's okay. Still playing the game, she tells me I got a raise, I can afford it.

The pizza costs $17.75 of the money Sylvia left, and I have to tip the delivery guy another dollar. It's worth it, it's a great pizza.

"I thought this was one of Sylvia's days off," Karen says while picking off the broccoli on her share of the pizza. "Did she change her days?"

The question is sudden. We haven't been talking about Sylvia.

"I thought I told you, she changed jobs."

Karen reaches for another slice of pizza. She doesn't look suspicious when she says, "Sylvia loved that job."

"Rocco is moving to Florida or someplace." That's true, anyway. "Sylvia gets to work a great big cash register, like a computer, at this new place."

Between bites, Karen asks, "Where is she working?"

Once or twice before we sat down to eat, I almost forgot Sylvia isn't really working late. I shrug, but I'm thinking fast. "It's a bus ride, then a change. I forget the name of the place. She gets home a little later, that's all."

"She still dating that same guy?"

Karen always asks about Sylvia's boyfriends. I say, "More or less," hoping she'll drop the subject.

"My mom said nice men never want to date women with children."

This is the only thing I envy Karen for. Her mom talks to her like she's another grown-up. "Why's that?"

Karen tosses her hair, a sure sign that she's about to make up an answer. "Too much trouble," she says.

"I try to be," I say. Even though Karen laughs, it doesn't feel like such a funny joke.

Karen tips her head back and lets the pizza cheese slide into her mouth. She is still chewing when she says, "So did you ask her?"

"Sylvia? Ask her what?"

"How old you have to be before you can date."

I did, now that she's bringing it up. Last week. It seems like last year. "Fourteen," I say, even though Sylvia's answer was fifteen.

"You're lucky to have Sylvia for a mom," Karen says.

"Yeah." I've lost my appetite.

When Karen pushes the pizza box away, she asks, "Hey, want to go put on makeup?"

"No." Sylvia has taken all her makeup.

Karen asks, "Why?"

I'm tired. I'm in no mood to pretend. "I just don't feel like it. I'm too old to play dress-up."

"Well, that's nice," she says in a snotty tone. "I guess you're just unusually mature."

"I guess so."

Karen notices it's seven-thirty, gathers up her stuff, and says, "Tell Sylvia I'm sorry I missed her."

After she leaves, I count the money, figure out how long I can make it last. The answer is, not very long.

TEN

Sylvia's bank statement is in the Saturday morning mail. It's hard to make sense of the columns of numbers. Maybe there's two thousand dollars in the bank.

I didn't expect that.

I go out to the stoop to think. Sylvia keeps blank checks somewhere. I'm not quite sure what I can do with them if I find them. But I'm going to need money if she doesn't come home soon.

It's warm in the sun. Paulie is there. His pale face looks stiff with cold, his clothes have this brown shine to them. He looks as alone as I feel.

"How's your foxy mama doing?" he asks.

"She has a cold." He never calls Sylvia a foxy mama to her face. He's always Excuse me, ma'am, this, and Yes, ma'am, that.

He comes over and sits down next to me. I scoot away a little.

He says, "What you got there?"

"Nothing," I say, and push the bank statement into my pocket.

"Nothing always give you a face that drags on the floor

when you walk?" he says. He has this street way of talking, so that "what you" becomes "whachu." "Nothing" turns into "nuttin."

"Maybe I'm catching Sylvia's cold," I say.

"Good if she left you something," he says.

My stomach grabs tight. "What do you mean?"

"The fox. I seen her clearing out of here like her tail was on fire Wednesday around noon," he says. "She went with that white-collar type, one drives the big-deal Toyota. Some rich guy she found herself."

"She'll be back on Sunday," I say. "Tomorrow. They just went for a little visit, like a vacation."

"Uh-huh. And you're too old to need a baby-sitter."

"Well, I am."

Old Mrs. Wisner, who lives on my floor, comes across the street, pulling her shopping cart behind her. Paulie gets up to open the door for her. "Such a gentleman," she tells him.

When she's gone inside, he comes back to sit next to me. "So let's say you're telling me the truth," he says almost gently. "You run through your money already, that you're contemplating things so hard?"

Hot tears sting behind my eyes with a suddenness that embarrasses me. My nose starts to run.

"Hey, now," he says, quickly getting to his feet. "Don't go turning on the waterworks."

"I'm not crying!"

He digs into his pants. "I can let you have five. You can get by on that, can't you?"

"Yes," I say, shoving the money into my pocket. I take a deep breath. "Do you know how I can get a check cashed? Then I can pay you back."

"Have Sylvia sign it, that's all," he says. "She's home by Sunday, right?"

"Suppose she isn't. I mean, what if she's late?"

He cuts his eyes at me. "Uh-huh."

"Just suppose. Can I get it cashed?"

"That kind of thing ain't like skipping gym class," he says. "Banks check signatures, you know. They got computers that pick up the teensiest little difference. Forgery, that's what they call it when you copy somebody's signature."

I wait.

"You got something with her signature on it?" he asks.

"I think so. I can't copy it." Sylvia's handwriting is half print and half script, with odd spaces between the letters. I've tried to do it, just for something to do, but I didn't even come close.

He gave me a measuring look. "You bring it to me. I got some abilities."

"Abilities?"

"I can copy exactly," he says. "Exactly" sounds like "eggzackly." He says, "I could be a graphic artist, you know. I bet you don't even know what that is."

"I do too. They make signs."

"Sign painters make signs. Graphic artists design things," he says. "Business cards and like that. They make up their own designs for letters. You know. Print."

"You'll help me, then?"

"I'll help," he says. "If you'll do a little something for me in return."

"Like what?"

"Come for a little ride with me, I'll show you."

"Nope. No rides. Sylvia wouldn't like that."

"Don't even go there, little girl," he says, so disgusted with me that I'm embarrassed to have said it. "I got nothing like that in mind. We got to get to a place so I can explain myself."

I narrow my eyes at him. "How far? Can't we walk?"

"Eighteen blocks! We can take the bus. That okay with you?"

"You paying?"

"I'm paying," he says like I'm driving him nuts.

I get a knot in my stomach. I don't see any way to back out.

"I'm doing this," he says as we walk to the bus stop, "because I understand girls have to be careful who they hook up with. You going to be on your own. Girls on their own can amaze themselves how well they do. You got to stay independent, that's all."

The more he talks, the more scared I feel. I haven't thought about anything but hanging on until Sylvia gets back.

"You got to know who you can trust," he says. "You can trust me like a big brother. That's the idea I want you to get."

I cut him a look. I don't need him to tell me about trust.

"Unless you don't want to be on your own," he says. "Then you might just as well call children's services right now. Save yourself the trouble of being found out."

"You live with the super and his wife. You aren't their son, are you?"

"Nope. Children's services put me there," he says. "Once they get you in their grip, your life ain't your own."

I don't need him to warn me about children's services, either. Sylvia already wrestled with this lady from children's services when Sylvia wanted me to have someplace to go after school. It ended up Sylvia said we can do without their help.

"You don't get a say about what kind of family they stick you with," he adds.

"You don't like living with Mr. and Mrs. Loach?" I ask.

"Now, that would qualify as my business," Paulie says as we get to the bus stop. "But since we're becoming so friendly—"

"We aren't friendly," I say.

Paulie lets maybe half a minute go by before he adds, "Living with the Loaches, it's better children's services come around pretty often. So I do things to keep them interested. Like cut school once or twice a week."

"Why?" It's a reasonable question.

He gives me a hard-eyed look. "Here comes our bus," he says. He doesn't answer my question.

ELEVEN

We take the bus to the other side of Washington Heights. Paulie talks the whole time, telling me the entire story of this movie he likes.

It's about a girl who needs to stop the man who killed her father, and she goes to this old gunfighter for help. She sees people shot dead, she gets kidnapped, she falls into a snake pit, and still, she wins in the end.

He tells a good story. And I get it, what he's telling me. The story of a girl who goes out on her own. Amazes herself, even. He's finished the story when he yanks the cord to stop the bus. It's a quieter neighborhood we've come to.

There are higher hills, some regular houses squeezed in between the apartment buildings, and Paulie says if we walk a couple of blocks more, we can see the Hudson River. But we aren't here to look at the river. We're here to look at a building.

Right away when we get there, he starts talking out of the side of his mouth like someone's trying to listen in.

"Rich old lady lives in this building. Goes out every Tuesday morning at eight-fifteen. Walks to the subway. Rides to Thirty-fifth Street to check on her money. She visits her sister at this fancy little old folks' home, like a boarding school for grannies. Same every Tuesday."

"How do you know so much about her?"

"I been following her around, that's how."

"Why would you follow her?"

He gives me a long look that says I might not be as smart as he thought.

"What's it got to do with me?" I want to know.

"I got a little project you can help me out with."

"Nuh-uh. Not me."

"It's one Tuesday. In return for which I sign your check. It's up to you."

"I'm in school on Tuesdays."

"I'll write you a sick note, okay?" he says. "It has to be Tuesday because that's her bank day."

He hasn't told me the plan and already I don't like the sound of it.

"And while we're on the subject," he says, "don't miss any school except that day. Make sure you wear clean clothes and brush your hair, stuff like that."

I ignore these instructions. "Why'd you pick her exactly?"

"Way she dresses. The coat she wears in winter? It's soft like a baby's bottom. Costs money to buy wool like that. Gray suede billfold to pay for her milk and eggs. That old lady has money she doesn't know what to do with."

"Sounds to me like she knows what to do with it."

"She's got enough to share, that's what I'm saying. I just want the loose change, that's all."

"Not me. No way."

"I got a plan," he says. "I'll tell you about it. Let's walk back to the bus stop. We don't want to be seen around here together."

We walk away fast. I'm sure I'm already guilty of something.

"It's very easy," he says when we round the corner. "You wait by the elevator and when she comes in, you ride with her to her floor. She lives on the fifth floor."

"You've been up on her floor?"

"I have to know where she lives, don't I? She's going to turn left, you turn right. You stop at the first door you come to and act like you ring the doorbell. Don't really push it, now."

"I thought nobody was going to be home."

"Nobody should be. Anyway, you don't ring the bell. You act like you rang and nobody's home. You run down to where she's gotten her door open. She's slow, so you'll have time. Wait until her door is open."

"No way—"

"You rush over, very agitated-like, and you say, 'Can I use your phone? You gotta let me use your phone.' Don't wait for an answer, just rush on in."

"Into her apartment?"

"Yes! Whaddya think? She's old and she's slow, so she can't keep up." He gives me an impatient glance. "You rush in, look for the bedroom, that's where old ladies keep their money. You open the top dresser drawer and slide your hand under the clothes."

I feel sick.

He goes on talking fast and low. "You don't find money, shut the drawer and get over to the bed table. Pick up the phone and talk into it, like all this time you been dialing. Put yourself between the door and the bed table. So she can't see you're in the drawer."

"I can't do that," I whisper.

"Once you find money, get out fast. Take the stairs. Or the elevator might still be there. Come here, where we are now. I'll be waiting for you in old man Loach's car."

"I can't."

"That's what you think now. You have to live with the idea a day or two before you give me an answer."

He's one of those people who doesn't listen. "No. Just no."

"You got something religious against stealing?" Paulie asks.

"I'm not doing it." I'm walking as fast as I can, nearly running.

"You're scared, that's what—"

"Yes, I am. Aren't you?" I stop suddenly, turn to face him. "If you really did this, weren't you scared?"

Without any of the stuff he usually puts on, he says, "All the time."

I believe him. I start walking again.

"Listen, how far you think you're gonna get without money?" he says, coming along beside me again. "Rent's due next week. You're on your own now, you have to make a living."

"Stop it!"

"I ain't asking you to do anything I haven't done myself," he says angrily. "I did this for five years and nobody caught me out, nobody ever came knocking on my door. I made good money. Excellent money. I'm too old now. Too tall. Nobody'll let me in their apartment without screaming the house down."

"You said nobody would be there."

"Uh-huh, that's right," he says, calm now. Friendly. "You're thinking now. That's good. You're thinking it over."

"No, I'm not."

He says, "You're a good pick for a business partner. You're small. People not around kids a whole lot, they guess you for nine or barely ten. Old people trust small."

I won't speak.

"I'm a good pick, too," he says. "You only gotta give me a chance."

I don't say another word the whole bus ride home. Paulie doesn't, either. He's wrong, I'm not thinking anything over.

He takes me back to the stoop, reaches as if to open the door, but he holds it shut. "It's a risk. I won't kid you about that," he says. "Everything carries risk. Run to catch up, you can fall. Cross the street, maybe you'll get hit by a car."

I hate everything he's saying, but I can't stop listening. "Go to sleep, you might not wake up."

"Sylvia's coming back."

"Where there's risk, there's chance. Nearly always, it's the chance that makes us take the risk. You want that chance?"

Somehow he's turned the words all around.

He says, "Just say yes."

I get angry so suddenly, the fierceness of it swells in my throat. "I hate you," I tell him before I go inside.

TWELVE

I hate being in the apartment alone.

I turn the TV on and off, mostly leaving it on so the place doesn't feel so empty. I know that only a few days ago I liked it, having the place to myself, at least I liked it in the morning. In the evening, I could pretend things that made it easier to wait for Sylvia to come home. There's nothing to pretend now, I don't feel like playing games.

The phone rings once.

That's it, rings once. I don't even have a chance to answer it. My guess, somebody who realized they made a mistake and hung up.

There must be something to do on Saturday afternoon, I just can't remember what it is. Dishes. The sink in the bathroom looks kind of scummy and the bathtub has a ring. The bathtub is the hardest work I have ever done in my life. I'm so glad the toilet has blue water.

I can't get Paulie off my mind. Wondering how many old people he's robbed. Wishing I'd asked him how Sylvia looked when he saw her. Like, was she happy.

And just when I'm almost not thinking about him, I remember I liked it when he called me a business partner.

I work out a way to brush my hair, lying on my stomach with my head hanging over the edge of the bed so my hair hangs down. This way, my arms don't get so tired and achy. I can even do a ponytail this way, although I mostly leave my hair loose now. All I have to do is roll onto my back before I sit up. My hair looks just as good as when Sylvia brushed it out.

I sit down to surf the movie channels, watching three of them at once.

Around six-thirty, the phone rings. "Hello?"

There's only silence at the other end.

"Hello?"

Nothing. I hang up, like Sylvia always told me.

In the next instant, I snatch the receiver off the cradle. "Sylvia? Sylvia, is that you?" My whole body has gone tight. There's only the dial tone in my ear. I hang up again.

Right away I grab a pen and do like the commercial says, dial *69. I write down the number. It's long distance, but I dial it anyway. Somewhere, a phone just rings and rings. A tape comes on to tell me no one is answering, like I wouldn't already know, and I hang up.

I hope it was Sylvia I hung up on. I want it in the worst

way, because I want her to call back. I'd ask her to come home. When the phone doesn't ring again, angry tears burn in my eyes.

I hope she's all by herself somewhere.

THIRTEEN

There's another call like that on Sunday morning, early. I pick up, there's a silence.

"Sylvia?"

I hear a click, and some recorded voice asks me if I want to buy awnings for my windows. I listen for a minute or two because I'm afraid of how I'll feel when I hang up.

Two big tears have to be wiped away, but that's it.

I have to go out for milk, and I tell myself I'm fine. Well. Almost fine.

I don't even mind that Paulie's hanging around downstairs like he's waiting for me. He falls into step beside me and tells me we ought to go back one more time so he can point out the old lady to me.

If I play along, maybe he'll sign that check, so I get on the bus with him. He doesn't ask about Sylvia, and I don't bother to pretend. We take the bus again.

He knows all the old lady's habits, like how she comes out for her newspaper so early in the morning, the sun's only just up. I have a picture in my mind of what the old lady is like. Rich and mean. Sort of a cross between Cruella De Vil and Mrs. McCrumb, my fourth-grade teacher, who had this big white car.

Then Paulie points her out to me.

She looks like somebody's grandma. "You didn't tell me she walks with a cane."

"Walks all day some days, with that cane," he says as if he admires her. "Can you beat that? She got grit."

"You're robbing an old lady who walks with a cane?"

"That's what makes her a good pick, especially you being a beginner and all," Paulie says. "Whaddya want, somebody who can chase you?"

"I'm not doing it."

"Now don't go getting cold feet," he says. "Nobody's gonna chase you."

"I can't do it."

"Trust me."

I walk away fast.

He's right behind me. "You gotta do it," he says.

"I'm going to be late." I expect him to say, late to where? I have a smart answer ready. When he doesn't say anything, I look over my shoulder.

He's gone.

I keep going. When I'm only a few blocks from home, I notice this woman walking ahead of me by about half a block. I've been watching her without thinking about it, because I have my mind on Paulie and all. I'm watching her more closely all the time.

She walks like Sylvia.

She's wearing a hat that covers her hair. She holds a pocketbook under one arm, like Sylvia does. The way her coat swings, she has some rhythm similar to Sylvia's.

"Sylvia!"

She doesn't turn around.

I don't know if I really think it's her when I begin to run. When she turns a corner, I run faster. I've lost her.

There's only one building where she could have gone. The outer door is unlocked. There's a small entry hall and then an inner door that is locked. This door is glass, with a curtain. I can't see through it.

I push a couple of doorbells, hoping someone will buzz me in.

I bang on the door. Try again to peer through the curtain.

Outside, there's a space between two buildings where garbage cans are kept. I run down the steps and all the way to the back of the building. I find a service entrance, but it's locked.

Walking back to the street entrance is hard, I keep wanting to sit down and rest.

Sylvia would have looked back when she heard me call. She would have. So why can't I shake the feeling that it was her?

Only one bell doesn't have a name in the slot. I ring that bell for a long time.

After a while, I go home. I want to talk to somebody, tell somebody. The only person who feels right is Paulie. The thing I want to tell him is, I can't take being so alone.

FOURTEEN

When I get home from school on Monday, Paulie's waiting for me again. I hate the way my heart gives a little leap. I hate even more the way it falls when he lets me walk by.

No, he follows me into the elevator. Pushing the buttons for every floor, he says, "This what you're going to wear?"

I shrug. Don't argue. I don't think I could stand to have anyone mad at me right now, not even Paulie.

Between the second and third floors, he says my jacket pockets are too small. I should be sure to tuck my shirt in so I can push the money down my neckline. That way my shirt will be a big pocket, the money won't fall out.

After the elevator closes on the third floor, he tells me my jeans are too tight. To keep my hair tucked inside my jacket. I don't want to ask why. I don't even want to think about it.

He has a route all mapped out for me to walk. I should cut between buildings, through the playground, down an alley. He talks when the elevator is between floors, falls silent when the doors open.

"Why can't I take the bus?"

Walking, he says, is safe. I won't be in one place long enough for anyone to ask what I'm doing out of school.

"Why aren't you coming?"

"I am," he says. "I'm going to be parked where I showed you the other day."

"That's not very close."

"Nobody's going to be chasing you, don't worry," he says as we get back to the third floor. "Just wear looser pants."

The elevator opens at my floor. I'm hoping he has more to say. When he doesn't, I try to look like I don't care. I even walk to my door like I can't get away fast enough. He holds the elevator door and waits.

Just as I'm about to step into the apartment, he offers, "I got some time to practice Sylvia's signature, if you got a copy."

Old papers are in the back of a drawer in the kitchen. The canceled checks that came with the bank statements have Sylvia's signature on every one. He wants a sample of the rest of Sylvia's writing, too.

Back in the living room, we find Sylvia's phone book in the table by her chair. Her phone book is all in print. I shuffle through a lot of paper until I reach the bottom of the drawer.

There isn't even an old grocery list. I hate Sylvia. I yank the drawer out and turn it over, letting everything spill onto the floor.

"Hey, hey, take it easy," Paulie says. He goes through the

mess, turns over what looks like a notepad. It's a block of extra checks. While he looks through the rest of it, I go back and take the kitchen calendar off the wall. Sylvia kept a record of practically her whole life on that calendar. In script.

"Great," he says. He sits down at the dining room table.

After a few minutes spent studying Sylvia's handwriting, he does several lines of practice swirls and parts of words. Getting a sense of the patterns Sylvia made when she wrote, he says. He's just showing off.

"How's this?" He passes me a note for my teacher, excusing me for the day. It looks like Sylvia wrote it, and signed her loopy signature.

"How'd you do that?" I ask.

He just leans back in the chair, looking smug.

"So sign the check."

He shakes his head. "Not until."

"This is so easy for you—"

"Hey, don't think that way," he says. "You think it's so easy, you do it."

I snatch the note out of his hand.

"So," he says, looking over toward the dark and silent TV. "You gonna offer me a sandwich or something?"

"I've got frozen dinners. You have to make your own."

He leaves around seven-thirty, after going over the plan with me again. He has me saying my lines like I'm in a play.

My homework is ready to turn in on Wednesday. There's nothing left to do but go to bed.

Instead of pajamas, I put on my favorite T-shirt. Black with a big lime green frog and pink lettering that reads GIMMEE A KISS, BABY. I love that frog. He looks so sure he's a prince. I decide to wear it tomorrow. For luck.

FIFTEEN

I turn all the lights on when I leave so that when I get home later and look up, my windows won't be dark and lonely. I look back once from the street. A feeling comes over me, like I'm leaving my only safe place.

Every step, that feeling gets stronger.

I can't help wondering if Sylvia felt this way. Wondering if she's somewhere right this minute wishing she'd turned back.

Wishing I could.

I can't turn back. There's nothing there for me if I go back.

It's cold out, so I take the bus. I figure what Paulie doesn't know won't hurt him.

He said the old lady comes home around two or two-thirty. I get there before one. I go across the street to the little bodega to check the time.

I decide to wait here where the storekeeper's talking to some old guy with a newspaper under his arm. The old guy flicks the ash from his cigarette into the fold of his newspaper. I hang around for a while, eating a big bag of chips and drinking a mango nectar. Chewing is good. Nobody's asked why I'm not in school.

Finally, it gets to be one-thirty. I expect to have to ring

someone's bell to get into the lobby. I feel lucky when the door gives way to a push. Paulie told me to look for the elevator before I do anything else. To take a little ride.

An empty fountain is set against the back wall of the lobby. A set of three steps on either side of the fountain leads up to the elevator, hidden behind the wall. The elevator is the old-fashioned kind that has two doors, one that slides back when the elevator stops at a floor and another heavy one to push open to get out.

I'm nervous. Crazy with nerves. There's a staircase at the end of the mail room, I run up two flights before taking the elevator to the fifth floor. The old lady's apartment is left of the elevator like Paulie said, it's the only one with a doormat.

I listen at the door where I'm supposed to pretend to ring.

Nothing to hear.

Downstairs again, I sit on the steps in the lobby for maybe ten minutes, biting my fingernails. Then I do the whole thing again.

Finally, because I have nothing else to do, I look up the old lady's name on the panel of doorbells. Martha Clark. It sounds like a nice old lady name.

I'm sorry I looked.

I charge across the lobby and up the steps. Back by the elevator, I make myself work out a way to play hopscotch on the tiles. Jumping from pale pink marbly stuff to dark pink marbly stuff, skip the beige. An empty gum wrapper, folded tight, is my marker.

Hop left foot, hop left foot, both feet down, and hop right foot, hop right foot, both feet down. Turning to hop back over the same tiles, I hear footsteps. Rapid footsteps. A terrified thrill runs up my spine. But it's only somebody's maid. She passes me, hurries into the waiting elevator.

My breath is coming too fast.

The door closes. I watch the arrow over the elevator move from one number to the next. She gets off at the sixth floor. I go back to my game, throwing down the gum wrapper. Hop, hop, slap. Hop, hop, hop, slap.

After a few minutes a woman comes to the door of an apartment a little distance from the elevator. "What you doing there?" she asks. She has an accent, and for a moment I don't understand her. "You live in this building?"

Paulie has not prepared me for this question. "No, ma'am."

"Then what you doing here? You no supposed to be in here unless you live here."

My guess, she's the super, or the super's wife. I put on my most innocent face. "I'm waiting for my friend."

"What apartment she in?"

"I didn't ask," I say, hoping the woman won't ask me for a name.

"So you wait," she says. "No jump."

The woman goes back in before I can finish saying, "Okay." I turn around at a small sound behind me.

SIXTEEN

The old lady smiles and says, "Hello, dear. I didn't frighten you, did I?"

I think about running. About passing Paulie without so much as a look over my shoulder, running eighteen blocks back to the apartment.

Then what? a voice in my head asks. How will I pay the rent? How will I keep going until Sylvia comes back?

I push the elevator button.

The elevator is on the way down, fourth floor, third floor. And what about children's services, what about when they show up? that voice is asking.

I push the button three or four times more. "You're an impatient one," the old lady says. She says it as if she likes impatient people. "My sister used to be like that. Always in a hurry."

I yank the elevator door open when it stops.

Some guy in big glasses looks embarrassed to find me, and the old lady, waiting there. He gets off the elevator, led by a little dog on a leash. The old lady moves toward the elevator like she's used to people holding the door open for her. So I do.

There's a puddle in one corner. We pretend not to notice the elevator smells.

Seeing the old lady up close, she's like Paulie says. Her clothes are real nice. The scarf she has wrapped around her neck is made of some kind of hairy wool, light as air. She leans a little forward with both her hands resting on the cane, quiet, until the elevator stops on the fifth floor.

I rush to open the door and then hold it again while the old lady comes out. It hits me how stupid this is, me holding the door. All the time planning to rob her. It's not a good thing to think about.

"Thank you, child," the old lady says without looking at me.

I go to the right, she goes to the left. Things are going just like they're supposed to. I step up close to the door and pretend to ring the bell. Down the hall the old lady searches her pocketbook, comes up with her keys.

I wait, like Paulie said, for her to get the door open. I can't stand still, wait running in place, never taking my toes off the ground. The old lady's hardly made a move to go inside when I call, "Hey, lady, wait."

She looks at me.

"Nobody's home." It comes out just the way Paulie made me practice it over and over. I hurry toward the open apartment. "I have to use your phone. I have to call for a ride."

"Why—" the old lady begins. I rush past her.

The first room is like a dining room, there's the buffet and the china cabinet, filled with dishes and stuff. Just no table and chairs. Then, through a wide doorway, there's a big living room.

I can't help taking a long look at the piano at the end of the room, the top angles toward the ceiling like a boat sail. I never knew people had pianos like that in their living rooms.

There's a doorway on my left and it takes me into a hallway. There are too many doors, how am I to know which one?

Behind me, the old lady is calling. "Child," she's calling, and I can't think.

Panicking, I duck through the first opening, the very next doorway. It's another dining room, one with a table and chairs and another china cabinet. Roses in a bowl on the table, the smell of roses fills the room.

Beyond is the kitchen, a dead end.

Coming closer, the old lady is sounding more like Cruella De Vil. "Child, why are you behaving in this manner?" Afraid to face her, I hurry into the kitchen, thinking, I should be in the bedroom.

"Child, where have you gone?"

I drop down out of sight.

The old lady passes the doorway, goes on down the hall.

I get up. My heart's beating so hard, my head hurts.

I see money stacked on the table behind the vase of flowers, and two small boxes, white cardboard and red velvet. I'm sorry I found it.

"Child!" The old lady's banging with her cane. I have to do it now.

I grab the money and the boxes, stuff them down my shirt. The boxes fall to my waist, caught in the tucked-in shirt. The money doesn't slide much. I step into the hall and come face-to-face with the old lady.

"Oh," she cries, throwing up her hands like she's seen a ghost. Her cane falls.

I give a little scream, too, at the same time. I can't help it.

"Here you are," she says in a shaky voice.

I run.

Never even look at the elevator. I run to the stairs and down as fast as my legs will carry me. Fourth floor, third, at the bottom of the second floor I trip over my own feet and fall the last three steps.

I yell.

Then hit.

My left arm takes a lot of the fall and I roll back to slam against the wall at the foot of the stairs. My view of the stair-well is swallowed up by a black frame that shrinks until there's only a pinpoint of light. Then the darkness backs off.

I pick myself up and start down again. It's harder to run. My side hurts. My side, my arm, my elbow.

My legs feel weak and shaky.

I keep expecting to hear someone coming after me, but my breathing is the only sound, and the volume is turned up. Like it's coming through a microphone.

I get to the first floor. Run through the mail room and out to the lobby, down three steps, my legs feel weighted. Like I'm running through syrup.

SEVENTEEN

Outside, my head clears. Everything is moving fast, I'm moving fast. Downhill. A thought flashes through my mind, that Paulie thought of everything.

I see this guy getting into a car. He's wearing sunglasses and the kind of hat men wear with suits. Just noticing him slows me down. He gets back out of his car, his blue car, and opens the back door.

I've never seen the hat and sunglasses before, but the way this guy moves is so familiar, I can't take my eyes off him. That's what I recognize, the way he moves as he gets into the front seat again, leaving the car door open for me. It's Paulie.

He has the car running like he said he would, and when I fall into the seat behind him, he peels out like we're in one of those car races on Saturday afternoon TV.

He doesn't say anything.

I can't say anything.

My breath sounds wet and sticky. I don't feel too good. Wishing he had one of those cars where there's only a button to push, I roll down the window. Let the cold air blast me in the face. It's not enough. At the next corner, I say, "Pull over."

He keeps going.

"Pull over," I yell. "You better pull over."

He pulls over hard. I'm pressed deep into my seat and then slammed against the back of his seat. I yank on the door handle and nearly fall out into the traffic.

I catch myself, bend over and vomit on the street.

A car goes by fast, close. Just noise in my ears.

"Hey, hey," he yells as I begin to sink to my knees. "Don't get down in it."

He reaches back and grabs me by the arm, yanks me halfway back into the car. "You gonna heave any more, get back out. Stay on your feet."

So I lean on the car with the traffic whizzing past. Breathing hard and deep.

He calls, "You all right? Get back in and let's go. You don't need to advertise."

There are two women across the street. One is leaning out the first-floor window, the other watching from the sidewalk below. They've stopped talking to look at me. Us.

I go around and get into the front seat.

He gives me some napkins from the glove compartment. His hands are shaking.

"I didn't see you right off," I say. "You parked a little closer."

"Somebody was in the other spot," he says with a shrug. As he pulls out into traffic, another driver honks long and hard.

"I'm glad you didn't give up and go home."

"I know, I know," he says. "She was late. I started to wonder where you were, were you in trouble or something. So I was coming up to the fifth floor to see what was going on."

I didn't expect to hear nerves in his voice, so much chatter.

"If you were in trouble," he's saying, "I was going to pretend to be your cousin or something. I was gonna say I'd take you home and tell your mother. So they'd let you go with me. You know."

I do know, and it's the last thing I expected from him.

"Then I saw you coming." Like there'd never been any doubt, he says, "Everything went all right, didn't it? Didn't Paulie tell you it would be fine?"

"I didn't find the bedroom. Only the kitchen."

"Oh, no," he moans. "Why is that?"

"It's a bigger apartment than you'd think," I say, hoping he won't be mad. "Different than any apartment I've seen. I should have gone further down the hallway. I was scared. I wasn't thinking right."

"Okay, okay," he says. "The next one, it'll go better. Look, don't worry. I'll help you get your check cashed anyway, okay?"

"I got some money." I pull my shirt out to get at it. "It was on the table."

"Hey, good," he says. "A few bucks is better than nothing."

The white box falls out. A few bills. I gather up seven, maybe eight of them. All of them with a big *100* printed on them. "It doesn't even look like real money." The rest of it is caught up around my bra. I leave it under my shirt.

Paulie glances over. "Holy—" Somebody honks and he snaps back to his driving. "It's real enough," he says with a kind of awe. "I got a feeling you did good for a first time."

EIGHTEEN

Paulie says, "I don't want no truck driver looking down and seeing that. Scoop it up and sit on it, wait until we get someplace safe."

He drives the next couple of blocks in silence. I'm kind of numb. Relieved. It's over, I tell myself, and Paulie will sign the check.

He pulls into a Wendy's parking lot, picks a spot that's nearly empty of cars. "We ought to be all right here for a little while. Let's see what you got."

I turn away and reach down into my shirt for the rest of the money. Paulie counts it up. There was more money under my shirt than I thought. Maybe a dozen or so more.

"You hit pay dirt! You did fine, girl." He folds the bills, shoves them into the top of his boot. "What's in that little box?"

"I don't know. I just grabbed." I must have dropped the other one. I can't feel it anymore.

"Oh, now that's a pretty thing," he says, and lifts something sparkly out of the box. It kind of grabs color.

My breath catches. "Is it diamonds?"

"Nah. Diamonds would be in a much fancier box. This

box is from Macy's. It's glass or something." He shows it to me, a pin to wear on a blouse. What Fran would call a brooch. "See how it's cut like a prism?"

Sylvia would love the rainbow. "If it was diamonds, would you sell it?"

"No," he says. "There's only one thing to do with jewelry, and that's throw it away."

"Throw it away?"

He turns in his seat to face me, like he wants me to listen really well. "Here's the thing you got to know," he says. "You can't be greedy."

"I—"

"Greed gets you only one thing," he says firmly. "Jail time."

The words take my breath away.

He goes on, saying, "If you take jewelry, you got to sell it to somebody. They know who you are. If they know, it figures that before very long, somebody else knows. The cops only need to follow a trail of people right back to you. So you don't take jewelry."

I can't listen anymore, I've stopped listening. I see there's something he wants me to say. "Sorry."

"It's all right. It's like you said, nerves and all. And I didn't tell you, that's my mistake. So from now on, money only, okay?"

I nod, even though there won't be a next time.

I can't do this again.

If children's services want to come and get me, I'll just run off somewhere. Live in the streets or something, sleep in public places. People do it all the time. I can beg for money, pretend I lost my bus money. No one says no to kids. I can get enough money to eat that way.

My mind is churning out ideas. Why didn't these ideas come to me before? My mind froze for a while. Now it's running hot, like lava pouring out of a volcano.

"Well, hey," Paulie says. "We're in the perfect place to get rid of this. Sit here for a minute. You hungry?"

I can't eat.

Paulie's gone for only a moment, or so it seems to me. I must've just stared out the car window. I can't remember having a thought pass through my head. Once he comes back and there's the smell of food, I'm starving. I could eat hamburger after hamburger and never stop, the hole inside me is so deep.

He seems to know that's how it is, because he's brought back four big burgers. "Now if you're going to feel sick—" he begins. I grab one, unwrap it partway and begin to wolf it down.

"Hey, slow up there," he says. "There's plenty more where that came from."

So I try to chew slowly. After a few bites, I can almost taste the food.

He takes two bites and wraps up the pin with the rest of his burger. It goes into the bag with the fries and wadded-up napkins. Whistling a little, not a tune or anything, just a kind of sound under his breath, he crumples the bag. "Be right back," he says.

The first bin is pretty full. He walks off down the parking lot to another one, drops in the bag.

When he comes back to the car, he says, "We're going to have to be smart about this. We're going to have to think real hard about what to do."

"About what?" I'm still eating.

"We have enough here to pay your rent, for instance," he says, like he's talking to himself. "But if you pay your rent in cash, and Sylvia usually sends a check, somebody somewhere is going to wonder why. So we still have to send a check for that. We don't want to draw any attention to ourselves."

"Oh."

"The other thing, these are all big bills. Now the occasional big bill, that's no problem. A bunch of them like this, that's likely to attract attention." This is beginning to sound harder than he'd told me it would be. "Then, this old lady might report the theft to the police."

I'm wadding up the last burger wrapper. I'm feeling better. I've been listening while he was thinking out loud. "You said they never do."

"They don't. I don't think. The amount of money isn't usually enough to interest the police. This is two thousand dollars," he says. He stretches out the words *two thousand dollars* as if he thinks I won't understand any other way.

"So?"

"So, I usually come away with something in the neighborhood of five hundred. Usually less."

I don't argue the point.

"So the old lady must've been planning a trip," he says. "Sure. That's why the jewelry was there. So much cash. Maybe she's going on a cruise."

Paulie's figuring things out as he goes along. "She might report it," he says.

NINETEEN

"Paulie!"

"Hey! I'm leveling with you. Don't go all scared little kid on me. That's not smart. That's stupid."

I should never have listened to him.

"I want you to tell me how many people saw you," he says.

I think about breathing, about taking a deep breath. It's hard to breathe right.

"Where they saw you, what you were doing when they saw you," he goes on. "Think back and tell me everything."

"Too many people, Paulie," I say. I'm going to be sick again. "Am I going to go to jail?"

He gets that look, as if a dumb girl is something smart guys like him have to put up with. "They don't put little kids in jail, didn't I tell you that?"

I shout, "You said getting greedy would get me jail time."

"I'm just telling you what I know, like a teacher," he says, very calm. "I'm trying to make a point. That's why I said that about being greedy."

I just glare at him. After a minute, he softens a little. "If you're doing this when you're older, like if something hap-

pens to me and you have to figure out how to get along on
your own, you'll remember what I said."

"Sylvia's coming back. I'm never going to do this again."

"Yeah, well, in case she doesn't, you need to know this
stuff," he says.

"She's coming back," I tell him, although I've never felt so
uncertain of anything in my life.

His voice is almost kind when he says, "I'm telling you.
That's all. You're lucky you got me to tell you. I had to figure
everything out on my own."

"Are you sure about jail?"

"You're still a kid, nobody is going to put you in jail," he
says. "That's definite."

"What would they do?"

"Children's services," he says shortly. "For you. Me, I could
go to jail. They don't call it that, but that's what it is. So we're
going to be smart, and neither one of us is going to get
caught."

He looks at me differently for a moment. Like he sees a
partner.

"Got that?" he says.

I nod.

"So tell me who."

"There was the lady in the apartment who told me not to
jump. Oh, and somebody's housekeeper. She didn't even look
at me."

"What time did you get there?"

"Earlier than you said," I admit. "I couldn't take waiting at home."

"All right, I can see that," he says. "You were nervous. Next time, it's better you don't do that. Too many people get a look at you."

I look away.

"Nobody else, you're sure?"

"I went across the street for a few minutes." Only now does that seem like a stupid thing to do. "I bought a bag of chips."

He shakes his head impatiently. "You didn't listen to me."

"I know."

"And what's with this shirt? Did you have your jacket open? No one would forget this frog."

"I just didn't think. I'm not used to this."

"How long?"

"What?"

"How long were you there?"

"Until I ate the chips."

His eyebrows rise to touch the hair that hangs down a little over his forehead. "You stood around there eating chips? Are you nuts?"

I don't want him to be mad at me.

"Why didn't you get yourself a drink, have a little picnic?"

I can't meet his eyes.

"You did. You got a drink," he says with disgust. "How many people? Just a ballpark figure."

I'm getting confused. "A what?"

"A guess!"

"Don't yell!"

"Just tell me," he says. "How many?"

"The storekeeper and somebody else who was hanging around talking. And whoever came in to buy something. A few people, I guess."

He says, "The storekeeper, was it a man or a woman?"

"A man."

"Well, that's something. He wouldn't notice so much. Most women see a kid standing around someplace, they could list every birthmark. Even the ones hidden under clothes."

"You said nobody looks at kids."

"Nobody but storekeeps and their gossipy friends. I didn't tell you to go into a store, though, did I?"

I don't want to fight. "Paulie, you're scaring me."

"I hope so. Because you're scaring the juice out of me," he says. "Why didn't you do what I told you?"

I shrug.

"We're going to have to lay low for a couple of days. You'll go to school, then come home. You don't go out. That's the rule, you got that?"

A tear slides down my cheek.

"Not even for chips," he says in a hard voice. "Call for a delivery."

"Okay."

"If the old lady gets driven around the neighborhood in a police car to see if she can spot you, you don't want to be seen. They might even bring her around to the school to look into the classes. So keep your eyes down. See if you can wear your hair a different way, braids or something. And don't wear this top again."

I nod.

Paulie's smart. I just hope he's smart enough.

He pulls into a gas station to fill the tank. "We'll get change of one bill here," he says to me.

The next stop is a tiny neighborhood drugstore. He leaves me in the car while he runs in.

When he gets back, he says, "I told the clerk I was shopping for an old lady in my building." He bought two boxes of tissues, Pond's cold cream, and some paste for false teeth. "You want any of this?"

I don't.

"Now for the split. We did lots better than I expected." He opens a box of tissues and pulls them out so he can stuff the money inside. "I got expenses, so for now I'm just gonna give you the change from the gas station."

"How much is that?"

"The change? About eighty-eight. A little less."

"Eighty-eight dollars?" I've never had that much money before. But then, I never had fifty-five dollars, either, and that didn't get me very far. I say, "That isn't much."

He says, "Make it stretch as far as you can. Buy food. No toys or stupid stuff like that. I don't want to have to tell you that again," he warns.

He's beginning to act like he's way too in charge of my life. "What expenses do you have?"

"You saw it ain't cheap to run this car. How do you think I case the neighborhoods for old folks? And now we're going to have to work somewhere I don't know so good."

I'd argue about it, except he's looking at me the way Sylvia used to when she needed me to be really grown-up. I liked the feeling that gave me. I still like it.

He goes on, "Which might not be so bad. We won't have to worry about who we bump into on a street corner. So I'll be looking for a good neighborhood while you're sitting in front of the tube. Someplace with lots of old people and not too many cop cars around. Don't worry or nothing if you don't see me for a couple of days."

He sounds like he's going to disappear on me.

"Don't come looking for me at my place, either," he says.

I need Paulie. I don't look away, won't let him look away. He sighs, makes a show of giving in.

"You want to see me, leave a note in the laundry room on the bulletin board. The note should say, 'Party on Saturday night. Everybody welcome.' That's it. No 'Dear Paulie,' no date, no time or nothing."

Scared, my voice comes from deep in my throat, where I can't let myself cry. I sound ticked off. "That's it?"

"I'll check every day by six," he says, and I make myself stare hard out the car window. "When I see the note, I'll know to meet you there at eight that night. Okay?"

"Okay."

"Now repeat all the rules back to me. I'm not leaving room for more mistakes."

TWENTY

Back in our neighborhood, Paulie makes me duck down as he passes our building, and drops me off two blocks away. He tells me, "Go to school every day. And stay indoors after school. Order pizza and Chinese if the refrigerator's empty."

I almost don't want to get out of the car, but when he drives away, it's a relief. It's getting dark and there are a lot of people on the street now, coming home from work. But I'm alone and I want it that way.

My arms and legs feel so heavy, I want to sit on somebody's stoop for a while. Except it's too cold for that.

I walk so slow, Paulie's already in front of the building when I get there. I ignore him. I know I didn't want to leave him a little while ago, but now I'm mad at him. Everything is worse than it was yesterday and it's his fault, the way I feel.

I keep remembering the way the old lady looked, like she couldn't understand what was happening to her. She looked so scared. I don't think I'll ever be able to forget that.

In the apartment, everything is just the way I left it. The TV's on, so is the lamp. "I'm home." No answer.

I drop onto my bed.

All along, I've had this picture of Sylvia coming home and wanting to know how I got along. How I took care of everything. It used to be a nice picture. Just before I fall asleep, it hits me: I hardly thought of Sylvia all day.

I wake up dreaming that a police car is chasing me. Down on the street somebody's car alarm is going crazy. It's dark outside, but it can't be too late. There are plenty of lights on in the building across the street. I have to get up. Brush out my hair. Look like Sylvia's taking real good care of me. See if Paulie's excuse is still in my school bag.

I want to shower, too. When I take my shirt off, the other box falls out onto the floor. The velvet one. It got caught where my shirt was still tucked in at the back.

Trying not to notice how soft it is, I open the box and flick it shut almost immediately. It's a ring. Beautiful. The old lady's face flashes into my mind. She must hate losing it.

I should never have looked.

I throw the box into the bottom drawer of my dresser.

I run the water hot. I can't hear anything in there. No car alarms. No music being played too loud. The dark bruise on my arm doesn't mean anything, doesn't worry me. I don't even think. It's just me and the rush of the water. I stay there until my toes look like pale raisins.

My frog shirt is the first thing I see, getting out of the shower. I leave wet footprints on the way to the kitchen, throw it away. I never want to see that shirt again.

The best thing would be to take the jewelry box out to the incinerator, just get rid of it, the way Paulie did the other one. I find it on top of the framed picture of the grandmother I'm named after, a grandmother I never knew. Sylvia kept it for me, even though she didn't know her either.

I can't believe how much worse I feel.

The box is so soft, the color so beautiful. Inside, the stone is as deep red as the velvet. There are tiny diamonds, or whatever they are, all around that gleaming center. I've never seen anything like it. I know now why Paulie won't have anything to do with jewelry.

Jewelry is too personal. It reminds him.

TWENTY·ONE

I do just what Paulie told me. I pull my hair back into a ponytail and thread it through a baseball cap when I'm on the street. At school I take off the cap and clip the ponytail to the back of my head with barrettes. The hardest thing is handing Mrs. Zeller the note he wrote me.

Mrs. Zeller hardly even looks at me as she asks, "Better now?"

Karen thinks I'm trying out some new hairstyle without including her. She never even asks why I didn't come to school on Tuesday.

In the middle of Mrs. Blume's class I get so hungry—I didn't eat breakfast, that's why—I have to pass a note to Karen asking if she has candy or something. As usual, Leonard reads the note before he passes it to Karen.

Karen sticks it in her desk without even looking in my direction, and after a minute or so, it's obvious she isn't going to pass me anything back. So Leonard rummages around in his desk, finally coming up with a granola bar. He passes it to me.

Like Sylvia would say, chivalry is not dead.

I break the granola bar and pass half of it back to Leonard with a grin. It tastes like oatmeal cookies.

Right after the late bell rings, there's a lot of activity outside the classroom. At first I'm worried the old lady's come to the school, like Paulie said. It's only the custodians changing the light bulbs in the hallway. I keep my nose close to my desk anyway.

"Casey," Mrs. Lesky says later that morning. Mrs. Lesky is science. "Are you having trouble seeing your paper?"

I bounce up. "No. No trouble. I heard it's good for the eyes to read close-up." I thought of that myself. Paulie will be impressed.

Mrs. Lesky asks, "Where did you hear that?"

"Just someplace."

Mrs. Lesky writes some letters on the board and makes me read them anyway. I can read all of them, even the tiniest ones, so she's satisfied.

Karen acts mad for the rest of the day and then doesn't wait for me after the last class. On the way home from school, I stop into a little fast-food place and buy a dozen tacos. Karen loves tacos, and she isn't going to get even one.

It's only as I'm waiting for my order that I remember— Paulie told me not to stop anywhere. I can't help wondering if he'll really look for a note.

I go into my building through the service entrance so I can stop by the laundry room. My note reads the way Paulie said. An invitation to a party, no time, no place for people to come to.

I stare at the bulletin board for a minute or two, then put the note in my pocket. Deep down, I'm more afraid of finding out that he won't look.

I take the elevator to the lobby. Our mailbox is stuffed. There are circulars addressed to Occupant and Current Resident, junk. There are book- and video-club mailers. I love to fill those out, feeling like I can have anything I want.

And there's a really beautiful envelope, something special. As thick as a coupon mailer, it's dark blue with gold stars and crescent moons all over it. I tuck it into the outer pocket of my book bag so it won't get messed up.

It's getting harder to do homework. I feel more and more like there's no reason to bother. I spread my work out on the dining room table like I'm ready to get serious. There's makeup work from Tuesday, it has to be in by tomorrow. Even with the blue envelope to look forward to, I can't make myself do it.

I eat a few tacos, watch a cartoon show, all the time planning to do my homework right after. I want to do the picture report anyway, it might even be fun. A little channel switching turns up a program about tigers in the jungle. I can't resist watching that. Then I get some Ring Dings and watch a rerun.

About six o'clock, the doorbell rings. I'm still watching television. Sylvia put a little wooden stool near the door, the one I used to stand on at the bathroom sink when I was little. When I peer out through the peephole, Paulie leans in close with one eye, looking in. Eagerly, I take the chain off and open the door.

"Good. Can't be too careful," he says, coming inside. "I came to find out how you're doing."

"I'm okay." I go right to the table like I'm working on my report. I don't like that he's caught me watching TV. That he's always the one with important things to do.

"I expected to see a note from you," he says. "To check me out, you know?"

I struggle to look cool and then decide against it. "I'm glad you looked."

"We ought to get those checks signed," he says, heading for the table. Everything's there, the way we left it. He looks through the bills. There's the phone bill, the electric bill, and the gas bill so far. He practices Sylvia's handwriting for a minute, then sets to work.

I look busy, too, cutting and pasting for my report. There's a question I've been wanting to ask him. "How'd you get started doing this? Did somebody show you?"

"Nobody showed me nothing."

"Why, then?"

He glares as he licks an envelope and seals it with the heel of his hand. "I had my reasons." When he's gone through the bills, he addresses the envelopes in handwriting that looks so much like Sylvia's, it makes my throat hurt.

"What does your handwriting look like?"

"Right now, it looks just like Sylvia's," he says.

"No, I mean, really."

He glances at me like he's stumbled over some truth he didn't know was there. "This is all I can do right now," he says. "I can't switch back and forth. I can't get my own handwriting back right now unless I look at it like I did Sylvia's."

"I'll get stamps across the street."

He reaches into his shirt pocket and fishes out a small book of stamps. "A regular Boy Scout," he says.

I hand him one of my homeworks and say, "One more signature."

"What's this?"

"Lesky wants a signature on anything worse than a C minus."

Paulie signs, saying, "How could you get a D on homework? The answers are right there in the book."

"Just because you sign her name you don't have to give me the same lectures."

"Up to you," he says. "You can be smart or you can be a smart mouth."

I take a different approach. "It was pretty smart for a little kid to think up robbing old ladies. Where'd you get the idea?"

He shrugs. "It's not a new idea, you know, robbing people."

"Then why?"

He shrugs. And changes the subject. "Report cards are due soon," he points out, making my heart nearly stop. I've forgotten all about report cards. I'll need another signature. He says, "If Sylvia hasn't come home by then, bring it to me."

"You mean it?"

"What, about Sylvia coming home?"

"About signing her name."

He looks offended. "All we been through together, you think I'm going to hold that signature over your head?"

"I didn't mean that." It doesn't even feel like a lie. "I didn't know you gave any thought to report cards."

"Of course I think about report cards," he says. "What's to eat around here?"

I heat up a few of the tacos.

Paulie channel-surfs for a few minutes, then settles in to watch an old movie. There's something I'd like better on the other movie channel. He says he likes old movies best. He hardly notices when I pass him a plate of tacos.

When the movie is over, Paulie looks like he might be about to disappear. I ask, "You got any idea how mousetraps work?"

"You saw mice?"

I shrug. I don't want to tell him I'm bothered by noises at night. "Sylvia bought these traps."

"No problem," he says. Like he's wearing a badge that reads SON OF THE SUPER. "Where are they?"

He messes around with them in the kitchen for a while. It has a friendly feeling to it, all that snapping and swearing going on. When he finishes, he sits down on a dining room chair to watch me clean up my mess.

"You want to be careful to keep your grades up," Paulie says. "You don't want somebody getting suspicious, calling home to find out how things are."

"If my grades went up, they'd have something to be suspicious about."

"You're not a good student?"

I hate to admit it.

His eyebrows raised, Paulie says, "You look the brainy type, you know?"

I pretend I don't even hear that, crumpling the scrap paper.

"You two have a fight or something?" he asks.

"You mean, why did Sylvia leave?" I make a big deal of getting my books and papers just so.

"You think it's because she's mad at you?"

"Sylvia hardly ever gets mad." I rearrange my books, thinking, Sylvia gets her heart broken.

"Yeah. I could see, you didn't give her any real trouble. You're a good kid."

"I used to be," I mutter, lining my books up with the edge of the table. Smoothing my report.

"You still are. You need taking care of, that's all."

Sylvia always seemed to hear two voices, the one I meant

for her to hear and another voice that whispered in her ear, telling her my deepest secrets. Paulie's like that sometimes.

When I don't say anything, he adds, "Sylvia, too. You ever think of that?"

I stop fidgeting. "Think of what?"

"That she wants somebody to take care of her. Like you do."

"Sylvia's not a kid."

"Everybody wants that feeling. You know. That somebody cares. That somebody's looking out for them," Paulie says, looking away. "I don't think that changes."

I can see Paulie wants that feeling. I wonder how long it's been since he got to feel that way. I know better than to ask. So I say, "You think that's why she left? So the boyfriend will take care of her?"

"If she had asked you, would you want to go?" he asks, looking at me in an interested way. "I mean, suppose you came home from school and Sylvia said, 'Pack your bags. We're moving in with whatzis-name.' What would you say?"

"I wouldn't have any choice, would I? I'd still tell her I didn't like him."

"How about if she said he was moving in here?"

I finish scooping up my pens, drop them into my book bag. "I don't know."

"Yes, you do. Come on."

"My dad lived here. We were a family here."

"There's your answer."

"You're saying I didn't give her a choice."

"Maybe. I'm not telling you it's your fault. There's a difference."

I'm not so sure. There was this, well, not a fight exactly. I'd been kind of ignoring Sylvia, and because we were on the street and Sylvia didn't want to yell, she gave my arm a little shake. "We don't have to drive each other crazy."

I wouldn't give in. Sylvia said, "I hate it when you look like that."

I pulled away, asking, "Like what?"

"Like you're asking yourself how come you're stuck with me." I wish Sylvia hadn't picked that moment to read my mind. Because it was only for a moment that I felt that way. Only for a moment.

TWENTY·TWO

Paulie is back Thursday night, bringing pepperoni pizza.

I don't want to look like I might have been expecting him. Hoping.

I say, "What's this?"

"What's it look like? Dinner." He sets the pizza box on the table, looking at my video-club application. "Signing up?"

"I might." I snatch up the page of stickers and the rest of the paper, saying, "Who's to stop me?"

"Don't go away with that," he says. "Let me see what movies they got."

Later, when we've finished the pizza and we're talked out about movies, he says, "I know what happened to your old man—"

"My dad?"

"Sorry," he says. "I mean, your dad."

My dad died of a heart attack. Sylvia and I were watching TV when the phone call came. She kept taking deep breaths as she listened to the news. She said "Yes," and "I guess so," and "He would have wanted that," and I knew it was something bad.

Sylvia didn't cry until she had to tell me.

Like he had to get up his nerve to ask, Paulie says, "What happened to your mother?"

"She got hit by a car."

"No kidding."

I stare at him.

"Well, I mean, it's unexpected, that's all."

"What happened to your parents?"

"Oh, listen, I didn't mean to bring up stuff," he says. "Let's not get into our sad stories."

"Why not? It's something we have in common—"

"We got nothing in common," he says in a hard tone.

"We're both orphans, right?"

"That's a technicality," he says in a way that makes me feel I've overstepped. "The one big difference between your life and mine is Sylvia."

Now I'm angry. "Sylvia isn't here right now," I say. "And my parents are dead, too. That counts."

"You're right," he admits, and we won't look at each other for a minute.

Then I can't take it. I'm still mad but I'm about to apologize. It's the only way I can think of to go back to talking.

He says, "My dad OD'd when I was three. Then after that, a few months maybe, my mom got sick. She had AIDS. She turned me over to the state. She was afraid she might infect me."

"You never saw her again?"

"She always knew where I was," he says. "She didn't talk to me until I was about eight. I'd seen her around plenty of times. I never wondered why she always seemed to be around, no matter what neighborhood I was moved to. I didn't remember she was my mother until she told me. Isn't that weird?"

"How'd she know where to find you?"

"She had a friend who could find out."

He's messing with the video stickers again when he says, "My mother needed money for medicine," he says. "That's how it started. I was eight years old, you have to understand that. I was a kid. I didn't know for sure she would die no matter what, not that I would have done different."

"You gave her the money?"

"Everything, up until about three years ago."

"What happened then?"

"She told me she wouldn't be coming around anymore. She was too sick." He hardens his voice and adds, "And she told me to stop what I was doing before I got old enough to get into real trouble."

"That's it?"

"No, she told me to go to college even if I had to go nights or something, and make something of myself. So it wouldn't be a total waste."

"So what wouldn't be a total waste?" I ask.

"Her life. Mine, too, I guess."

"She loved you, Paulie."

He says, "How about we watch some TV? Maybe we could find a movie with a lot of cars racing around, something like that."

Even the movie isn't enough to keep me from thinking about how lucky I was to have Sylvia. Wishing I'd told her so, even once.

Things would have been different if my dad hadn't died. Sylvia changed, it was like she'd crossed a road, headed off in a new direction. She started reading to me every night, like she did when I was small. Sylvia still only wanted to read *Peter Pan*.

Even I changed. Not that I could see any difference if I looked in a mirror. It was like crossing the same road going the other way. I didn't feel like a kid anymore.

Paulie turns off the TV around eleven o'clock, saying, "What's bedtime around here, anyway? You aren't the sort of kid who takes advantage, are you?"

Once he's gone, I'm alone again. I remember the blue envelope. Instead of turning the television back on, I make hot chocolate. Take everything in to bed. The envelope is addressed to "Sylvai" in gold ink.

Inside, there are moons and stars all over everything, it's like opening a treasure chest. There's a booklet. And a folded-over page headed MYSTIC PYRAMID MEMBERSHIP APPLICATION.

On the back of the application, I read, "The lessons of the Mystic Pyramid have changed my life." And "My family is united again." And "You have brought so much blessing into my life, I cannot express in words my gratitude to you."

The skinny booklet reads, "Greetings! from the Mystic Pyramid."

If she buys, "Sylvai" will learn an ancient mental technique to open her third eye so she can go on to "exceptional attainments." There's a drawing of a face that shows an eye between the eyebrows.

She gets mystic teachings of the golden thread that binds all people together as one. The lessons explain the silver wave, which is how thought becomes reality. And they tell about the true meaning and mystery of redemption, and "more significant arcane knowledge."

It's probably not for real, but I want it.

I fill out the application, giving my name and address, and I make a big check mark in the box to indicate that I'll pay for all the lessons at once for the one-time low price of $79.95. I have enough money.

There are a lot of questions, too, like where was I born, what's my religion, and what do I do for a living. I fill it out truthfully, writing that I steal from old ladies. It feels good in a funny way, like I'm finally able to tell somebody.

The envelope doesn't have a stamp already on it. Not even

the printed-on kind, like most stuff that comes in the mail. The address, I notice, is only a few blocks away. That's pretty interesting.

Everything goes back into the envelope. I stick it in my sock drawer with all the video-club applications I've saved.

TWENTY·THREE

On Friday, because Paulie doesn't plan to stop by, I take twenty dollars and go out to get a bunch of movies. It's something I've always wanted to do. And I'm going to stop and buy ice cream at the corner store and eat it instead of dinner.

I get home two hours later with the ice cream and four movies that are so new, they haven't even come on cable yet. Halfway through the first movie, the phone rings.

I pick up in a hurry. "Sylvia?"

"She's calling you?" Paulie asks.

"No."

"Well, it don't hurt to keep up your hopes, I guess," he says. "I figure you remember I'm not coming by. You didn't have your girlfriend come over?"

"Karen?" I hadn't even thought of her.

"So what are you doing, watching videos?"

He's like a regular detective. "How'd you know?"

"I was driving past when I saw you come out of the rental place. So you won't miss me, huh?"

"Guess not." Like I could never miss him.

"Here, and I thought I was winning you over with my sunny personality."

"Keep trying. I like my pizza with extra cheese."

He actually laughs. That makes me feel good. When I go back to watching the movie, I don't feel quite so alone.

On Saturday afternoon, I'm eating lunch with the week's best mail spread out in front of me. Every so often I stare out at Sylvia's patch of blue sky.

I've filled out applications for another video club and a book club. Twelve movies for nincty-ninc cents and three free books. Sylvia loves bargains. And this patch of sky.

I asked her once what she thought about when she stared out like that. She'd answered, "Oh, I'm just wishing the window was bigger." Sylvia would have loved getting the blue envelope in the mail. She would have signed up, saying, "Something about that envelope has hope written all over it."

It does.

The address I'm going to is only two blocks away from the old lady's building. It feels like dangerous territory to me. The closer I get, the more my skin creeps, like an early-warning system.

It turns out to be an ordinary red brick building. Three floors, there are six apartments. I push a bell for the top floor and wait because there's no sign for the Mystic Pyramid. When the buzzer sounds, I go in.

It smells like every other apartment building I've ever been in. Odors from last night's dinner, stale cigarette smoke, a faint scent of mothballs. There isn't any mail room to look for. The boxes are all on the wall just inside the door. The second box reads C. WALIS—M.P. Mystic Pyramid?

I read the others, just in case. Wilenski, Tresta, Gleasow, Mayer, Aronson. The second box belongs to an apartment on the first floor. They still have the old-fashioned doorbells that turn like a windup toy. *Brring, brring. Brring, brring.*

"All right, hold your drawers up," someone says from inside.

The door opens and a short fat woman looks out at me. She's wearing a faded housedress, the kind Sylvia says a woman should not let herself be caught dead in. And a kind of hairnet. Under the net, her hair is a hard gray color. She doesn't say anything more, like, what can I do for you? She just looks at me like it's my turn.

I yank the application out of my pocket. "I got one of these a few days ago."

She gives me a sharp look. "So?"

"So, I wondered if this is where it came from. See, the address is right here on the envelope."

"You got a complaint?" Her voice is heavily accented.

"No, I'm not even a member. I'm thinking about becoming a member, I'm finding out more about it." I put the envelope back in my pocket.

She peers into the hallway behind me. "Anybody with you?"

"No."

"Your mother know where you are?"

"She thinks I'm at a friend's house, okay? I don't have to be home for a while."

She seems to reach a decision. "You want to come in for a while, we can talk."

"This came from you, then?"

"Your name musta been on the mailing list I bought," she says. She opens the door wider. Her apartment looks less like any old lady's apartment than I have ever seen. The couch sags in the middle. The coffee table is a board laid across two stacks of phone books.

When I take my jacket off, my hair crackles, stands away from my shoulders. It's worse when I try to smooth it down.

She takes me to the kitchen, where, with a wave of her hand, she tells me to sit. The table has rusty metal legs and a red and white top. It reminds me of a table Fran has in her basement, where she folds laundry.

I'd pictured everything differently. Not that I knew exactly what I thought I'd find—a churchlike building, or a storefront maybe, smelling of incense. Not this old lady. Not this run-down apartment.

She sits across from me. "So, what do you want to know?" she asks.

"I want to know exactly what people are grateful to you for." And because that might sound insulting, I add, "I want to know about the golden thread and the silver wave. Things like that."

"The golden thread, the silver wave, these are part of the course," she begins.

"I can pay," I say before I remember what Paulie said about showing the money around. "Your letter said I can pay for two lessons at a time."

"That's so," she says. Her eyes close when she nods, which makes her look like a big doll or a puppet of some kind. "As I was saying, I can't talk too much about the golden thread and the silver wave with someone who is not a course member," she goes on. "It's not as if these secrets can be had only by those who can pay for them, these are universal laws, the wave and the thread. The information is technical, you understand? You have to study."

Only now that it appears that the answers will not come so easily do I realize how much I'm counting on them. I need help.

"I am happy to offer the wisdom of the Mystic Pyramid Book of Life to those who are in need," she says. "So let's stick to specifics. What exactly is the problem that brought you here?"

I'm not ready to talk about that. Not yet. I read from my application. "Somebody wrote you they're able to walk again. Another person says they're cured of cancer. Somebody else—"

"Yes?" She's getting impatient with me.

"Is it mainly sickness that you can help?" I'm nervous, wadding up the application, finally squeezing it into a tight ball. "Are there answers to questions that are sort of hard to find words for?"

"The meaning of life," she says, sounding almost bored.

"What?"

"You are restless, longing for something beyond the ordinary," she says, and I can tell she's said it a lot of times before. "You want to know what is your mission in this life—uh, your purpose."

"Don't you think I'm too young to have a mission?"

"Everyone has a mission. It is my mission to help you find yours through the wisdom of the Mystic Pyramid. I am here to help you find real and lasting spiritual and emotional attainments."

"Yeah, the attainments," I say. "That's like going to school, I guess. Like you said, I have to study."

"School isn't everything," she says. I've never heard a grown-up say that. "It helps in this world, of course," she adds. "There are other worlds. Spiritual worlds. Occult worlds. In these worlds, intellect means nothing."

She rests her arms, her weight, on the table. Making herself comfortable. Which makes me feel a little better. I spin the balled-up application around under my hand while she thinks. Set it aside when she says, "Perhaps you are looking for forgiveness."

Forgiveness wouldn't be enough.

"I need another chance," I tell her. "That's what I'm looking for."

There doesn't seem to be any point in keeping secrets. "Sylvia, she's my stepmother, she went off and got married. I think. At least that's what she told her boss, Rocco. She told him we're moving." I take a deep breath. "Then she did. Move."

She doesn't need to have anything explained. "She left you behind."

"So then Paulie—" I hesitate, realizing I don't need to tell her about Paulie.

She nods encouragingly. "This Paulie, he's your brother?" When I shake my head, she asks, "How old is he?"

"Fifteen. Sixteen, maybe. He knows a way to get money, I won't say how. I needed money and he needed a partner."

"He takes some of your money?"

"It's our money." Eighty-eight dollars of it was mine, anyway. "We're partners. Only I don't want to do it again."

"How long since she left, this Sylvia?"

"Eleven days now."

"There are agencies for this," she says.

"Don't turn me in, please," I say.

"I don't plan to turn you in," she says, frowning. "How you gonna get along?"

"I'm fine." Although it hurts me to say so in some way I

can't explain. It's good we're moving on to a subject I've been thinking about. "I can baby-sit and walk dogs, small dogs, that kind of thing."

"That don't pay the rent," she says. "How old are you?"

"Twelve."

"In human history, there have been times when twelve was old enough." She shrugs. "There are parts of the world where that's still true. However, we are not in that time or place."

I figure this must be from the lessons. "What's the Mystic Pyramid got to say about that?"

She says, "The Mystic Pyramid doesn't recognize suffering, it knows only experience."

"What do you mean?"

"If you eat, it's an experience," she says. Then, spreading her hands before me, she adds, "If you starve, this, too, is experience."

"Paulie gives better advice than that."

"There is a saying. God helps those who help themselves."

"What's God got to do with the Mystic Pyramid?"

She just looks at me, there's no answer in her eyes.

"Sylvia will come back." Part of me still believes that.

She says, "She might not."

I was five years old when my dad met Sylvia. She was the most beautiful person I'd ever seen. She read fairy tales to me and she never pulled my hair when she combed it. I wished she could be my big sister. But I also hated her. I worried that when my dad married her she would turn into an evil queen. I was wrong.

"Sylvia thinks wishes come true." My voice comes out high and tight, my throat aches. My heart, too. "Sylvia claps for Tinkerbell."

"And you?" she asks. "Do you clap for Tinkerbell?"

"Sometimes." When Sylvia clapped real hard. The truth is, I always made Sylvia believe for both of us.

"Then perhaps you are right." And, as if we're talking about nothing of any great importance, she asks, "You hungry? You want something to eat?"

"No. I mean, no, thanks." A feeling takes hold of me, there must be someplace else I should be.

She leans toward me. "I will tell you something from the teachings of the Book of Life."

I'm listening.

"If you will have something, you must acknowledge it."

I don't get it. "Acknowledge?"

"This means to know it the way you know your own face in the mirror. You recognize it."

I wait, hoping she will say something more.

"Let us say," she says, "act as if it is already yours."

"Act like what's already mine?"

"This second chance. If you were sure of it, what would you do?"

"I don't know. I kind of have to let what you've said sink in."

It seems rude to just jump up and say, gee, it's late, gotta go. I stare hard at my fingernails for a minute, and think of what must be the right thing to say. "Do I owe you anything for this? Like a lesson or something?"

"Not necessary," she says with a wave of her hand.

"You know, you never told me what to call you."

"My name is Razza."

"Well, you've been very nice about the way I just turned up at your door." This is my voice that's like Sylvia's. I pull on my jacket. "You've been very helpful to me, too. I better get home. It'll be dark soon."

Razza watches as I let myself out. I feel like something under a microscope.

TWENTY·FOUR

It's much colder. Even ducking out of the wind now and then, it's the kind of cold that works its way through clothing. I'm thinking hard about everything the woman, Razza, said, when I realize—I left my application behind.

My heart nearly stops.

So stupid. I should have remembered to pick up the ball of paper. I never should have written down about robbing old ladies. Paulie would never have made these mistakes. I have to think things through, the way he would.

Razza might just throw it away. If I go back now, it's like saying, see, in case you didn't notice, I have something to be afraid of.

But if I leave it there, I still have something to worry about. Stupid, stupid, stupid.

Walking back toward Razza's building, rounding a corner, I slam right into a guy who's stopped to let his dog put a mess in the middle of the sidewalk. "Sor—" I've seen him before. It doesn't give me a good feeling, either.

He looks back at me the same way. It's the dog I recognize. The one that peed in the old lady's elevator. "Hey," the guy says in an uncertain way.

I run.

Sounding more sure of himself, he shouts after me. "Hey!"

It's a long block ahead of me. About halfway along, a sharp pain comes up my side. So sharp, I can't really run anymore. I look back. The good thing is, the dog won't run.

I keep going, though. Walking fast, running a few steps before I walk again. I head for a playground in the middle of the next block. Cut through to duck into the nearest building.

The doors are locked.

The building has one of those tunnel-like throughways where the garbage cans are kept. There's a row of maybe eight huge plastic cans. I run down the few steps, duck down behind the last one.

After maybe half an hour I hurt from the cold. When I'm not worrying that I hear him coming, I can only think of Sylvia, how I wish I could go home and tell her about all of this. She could almost always make me feel like tomorrow would be better.

After what I think must be nearly an hour, I ache with cold. It must be safe enough to go home.

I keep looking ahead and behind and checking around corners before stepping out to cross the streets. I'm going to wait for Paulie in the laundry room. No way I'm leaving a note and waiting for him to see it.

Pretty Mrs. Gonzales from the fourth floor is there. "Casey, *querida,* where you and Sylvia been? I han't seen you in days!"

"Sylvia got a new job. She's been putting in a lot of over-time." It's getting to be an old story.

"She's working in a office, is that it?" Mrs. Gonzales is stuffing her laundry into the machines as she talks. She talks like she's puckering up for a kiss. That's how Sylvia puts it.

"About time," Mrs. Gonzales is saying. "A woman like Sylvia, she's too good to work as a cashier. A woman has choices these days, she can choose a serious career path, you know?"

Now that I'm standing still, shivers keep running through me. I lean against one of the dryers that's working.

"Plus, she'll have better hours," she's telling me as she surrenders her quarters to three washing machines. "Got to go across the street for more quarters for the dryers," she tells me. "You gonna be here a few minutes?"

"Sure."

"You're a sweet thing," Mrs. Gonzales says, and pats my cheek as she goes by. She frowns at me. "You should come in outta the cold a little sooner."

I sit down in one of the plastic armchairs. It's five minutes, maybe less, that I have to wait. Paulie glances in at the board, then sees me. I can't help crying.

He glances around to make sure we're alone. "What's wrong?"

"I forgot one, Paulie. A guy got off the elevator with his dog while I was standing there with her."

He gets it right away. "Where'd you see him?"

"I bumped into him on the corner by the bean tree." Every kid in the neighborhood knows that tree. "He yelled after me, but I ran. I hid behind some garbage cans and waited an hour before I came home. I didn't see him again."

"You did good," he says. "But I don't like that he knows you live around here."

"What are we going to do?"

He doesn't answer right away. He's thinking. Still, two or three minutes is all I can give him. "Paulie?"

"It takes more than thirty seconds to solve these kinds of problems," he says. He doesn't sound mad. "You need a disguise."

"A disguise?" A mustache and sunglasses comes to mind. Paulie is looking at me very hard.

"We gotta give you a haircut," he says.

I reach up to protect my head as if scissors appeared in his hands.

"It's the easiest way to make you look different."

"Forget it. Sylvia would kill me if I let you make a mess of it."

He just looks at me.

"She could still come back."

"All right, I'll take you to a barber."

"Why a barber?"

"Because your mother would take you to a salon," he says. "Because the mother who would send you out with your brother or your cousin wants it done on the cheap. And barbers are cheap. At least they're more cheap than the beauty parlor."

It's hard to argue with Paulie's logic.

TWENTY-FIVE

The first two barbers want to know if this is all right with my mother. One says she has to be there if he cuts my hair. Going from barber to barber, Paulie does the talking. He can act real tough, like he used to do with me, and like a big brother disgusted with the way his day is going. Or he can be awfully "very nice boy" sounding, the way he used to be with Sylvia.

Lately, when we're together, he slips into this place between the two. Every so often he sounds, well, regular.

After the third barber, he pulls me into a store and buys two packages of gum. He doesn't even ask what kind I like. "Chew," he says, handing one package to me. I chew.

He wraps some of the hair at the back of my head around his wad of gum. When he drops it, it hits my shoulder. I take my gum out of my mouth.

"Smush the gum in," he says. "Make it look like you fell asleep with gum in your mouth."

"Only a crazy person would have this much gum in their mouth." But this is an emergency and I don't have any better ideas. I press the gum in over my ear.

"That's it," he says approvingly, which doesn't make me feel one bit better. "Let's go find another barber."

The next barber says I can sit in the chair and we'll talk about it. "See how close to the head it is over here?" He uses the scissors to point to the gum over my ear. It got pretty cold while we walked around looking for another barbershop. Now it looks like it's always been in my hair. "Going to be awful short," he says.

I see he's right, I didn't think of that when I put it there.

"Her mom said that will be fine," Paulie says. As if he'd actually given the problem of my hair some thought, he adds, "She's tired of brushing it, you know?"

I throw a mad look Paulie's way. Paulie doesn't even look sorry.

The barber cuts away the gum, then he cuts hair from the other side so I match. It looks pretty bad. I look down. I won't let myself cry.

The barber says, "You're sure about this, now?"

"We're sure," Paulie says, like, let's get on with it.

The barber goes on cutting. I watch the hair pile up on the floor. More long pieces, then shorter fluffy pieces.

I'm mad now, but not at Paulie, not anymore. This is all my own fault. I have to have a rule from now on. There's a time to say yes and a time to say no. And either way, I have to stick to my word. I have to. Even if I'm scared.

I can feel the scissors close to my head, snipping, snipping. I've stopped watching the hair fall. I don't look at myself even when he tells us he doesn't know much about cutting women's hair. Paulie says, "Lots of those fancy run-way models, they have these haircuts could have come from barbers. Probably did."

I figure I'm ruined. I'm ruined and he's feeling sorry for me.

The barber finally goes over the back of my neck with a little shaver that sends a buzz clear to my toes. I peek up, catch sight of myself in the mirror.

I'm not ruined. My hair lays flat, coming to little points all around my face, like I'm wearing a bathing cap. I hardly recognize myself.

"Look at those eyes," the barber says when he snaps off the shaver. "Big as stop signs."

"Yeah," Paulie says as the barber dusts off my neck with a big soft brush.

I see Paulie's thinking about that, probably planning how I should look down all the time. And as if to prove I'm right, he makes me go back to the apartment. Takes me back like I'm a stray dog that can't be trusted not to wander off again.

He looks like he hopes I'll want him to stay. I do. "Are you hungry?" I ask.

"Me? No. Do I look hungry to you?"

"Sort of."

"Well, I'm not. If I was, I have money to eat."

"I know that." But he goes off looking annoyed and unappreciated.

I should have told Paulie I wanted him to stay a while. Let him feel like he was doing me a favor. If he has to admit he needs something, he doesn't like it. I know just how he feels.

I'm alone again and I'm sure I feel worse than he does.

I go into the kitchen and right off I see I've caught a mouse.

"I'm sorry," comes out of my mouth before I can stop it. The mouse looks cute, shocked, and dead, all at once.

TWENTY-SIX

On Sunday morning, I turn my head on my pillow and wake up fast. My head feels so light, it kind of scares me. I get up and look at myself. It's like I never knew the shape of my head before. There was a face shape and a hair shape. Now there's a head shape that was there all the time, hidden.

After about ten trips to the mirror, my head stops being a strange sight and I see something sort of naked in it. Not the kind of naked that needs covering up, but the brave kind, like trees in winter, and caterpillars, and wet stones.

There's so much air around my ears that I feel almost graceful. I bound out of the bathroom in great leaps, circle the room and then the dining table, never bumping into anything. Leaning against the wall, I slide down and sit there, my heart pounding.

It's not just a feeling. I am different.

When I go into the kitchen, the first thing I see is the dead mouse. I won't touch it. After a moment, I open up a paper napkin and cover it up. It's not enough, though. No way I'm going to sit there and eat breakfast.

I'll eat out, the way Sylvia and I used to do. Of course, we always went to Rocco's. I have another destination in mind.

I go through my pockets, counting money. I'm going to have to ask Paulie for more money soon. I take the train uptown and into the Bronx, just the way I used to do with my dad.

I don't remember that it's such a long trip. The woman who sells me subway tokens gives me directions to the zoo. Once I'm through the gate, I remember where to find everything. First are the plains where there's elk and buffalo.

The plains go on and on. It's cold, but I notice the trees are getting tiny green tips to the branches. Spring is coming.

I go straight to the building with all the parrots and love-birds flying free. The place looks like a jungle. I spend most of the day here, where it's warm. Sometimes it's almost boring, but then a rainbow-colored bird will fly past. I think of the bluebird of happiness and how maybe he really is yellow.

Or maybe he's a she, I wonder if Sylvia ever thought about that.

I keep touching my head, surprising myself again. Measuring my hair with my fingertips. I get it now, what Sylvia likes about coloring her hair. This feeling of being changed. Of it being possible to change. And even of change being a good thing.

I remember the day after Thanksgiving, it turned out to be the last warm day before winter. It was practically hot out and I'd spent the afternoon in the playground. When I came up to the apartment, Sylvia asked me to go back down and get her some hair color from the drugstore.

She gave me the color and the number exactly. She said, "It's a little lighter than I usually go. I feel like I'm having more fun today, I ought to be a little more blond to match."

We both laughed. I didn't even get the joke, it was just good to laugh with Sylvia.

The boyfriend, Jim, saw the box in the waste can the next day. He asked me where it came from. I said it was Sylvia's hair color, because what else would it be? I didn't get it that he was going to be mad if it was a new box.

He said Sylvia had promised to let her hair go back to being brown. He threw the box down on the kitchen floor. An empty bottle broke, and scattered across the floor. That was when Sylvia came in to see what was going on.

Our eyes met for only a moment before Sylvia lied. She said, "That's an old box. I didn't want to waste it, that's all."

He didn't even help us clean up the glass.

For just a second I wish I could see him living with Sylvia. He'd hate it when she painted his walls blue and then peach and green and lavender and pink, like in our living room. The idea makes me grin.

My stomach growls and I go out to find some food.

Hanging out near the stand, eating two hot dogs, I think up more reasons why Sylvia would want to come home. She would have her own room. She could have first pick of which movie we watch. I'd clean the bathroom.

And she could dye her hair purple if she wanted to, I wouldn't say a word.

I throw the last of the bun and the paper into a waste-basket. When I turn around, the old lady's face is right in front of my own.

I snap back to attention so fast, my neck cracks.

The old lady's really here, leaning on her cane. The hair-cut doesn't fool her.

For a second I don't move. Don't think.

"You," is all she says.

And then I run.

Panicked.

I run back toward the bird house, from there toward the grassy plains. All the way praying that I'll be able to find the gate.

Reaching the place where I noticed the green tips on the trees, I look back. No one's following me.

I slow to a fast walk. Try to think.

I've already made a bad mistake, running away. Probably I should have just walked away. Even walking fast like this tells anyone who looks that I'm guilty of something.

Then again, the old lady might have yelled while I was running. It could happen that I didn't hear her. So maybe running was the right thing to do. Just that thought is enough to make me run again. That thought and the sight of the gate up ahead.

Once outside the zoo I run across the street, not even checking whether I have the light. Whether I could get hit by a car. By the end of the next block it hurts my throat to breathe. The cramp in my side is back.

I stop running because I have to.

I limp the rest of the way to the subway, breathing in great gulps of air. People on the street look at me as they go by. I try to smile so it'll look like I've been playing some kind of game.

Once I'm on the train, I decide not to tell Paulie the old lady saw me. I don't want to talk about it. I hope he's around somewhere so I can invite him up. If he's keeping me company, I won't have to think about it either.

The laundry room is empty, the lobby, too. He's nowhere around. Back in the apartment, I get a bag of cookies, turn on the TV. Concentrate on the TV.

The doorbell rings after I've been home for about half an hour. I think to myself, there's Paulie.

TWENTY-SEVEN

When I open the door, Razza is standing so close that she fills the doorway. She's not alone. There's a younger woman looking over her shoulder, a dumpy-looking woman with greasy hair and a hungry expression.

"This is my daughter, Sasa," Razza says, and pushes past me, her dark coat brushing roughly over my face as she comes in. "I came to see how you're getting along."

"I'm fine." My heart is beating faster than ever.

"Do you have everything you need?" Razza asks, her sharp eyes moving around the room. Her voice is friendlier now that she's in the apartment. But that's just a mask she wears. "Anybody been bothering you? You could close the door."

"I'd rather leave it open, if you don't mind."

I sound so polite. I haven't let go of the doorknob and I'm not sure I can. Sasa's walking around, looking at things, looking into the kitchen. She's about Sylvia's age, but there's something strange about her, she looks old and young at the same time.

Going through my room and then going into Sylvia's, Sasa isn't scared and wild like I was at Mrs. Clark's. She moves slowly, feeling sure of herself. Like everything she touches is hers for the taking.

She noisily opens drawers and closes them in Sylvia's room. I'm shaking with anger and helplessness. "You better leave now."

Razza's eyes flicker over me, then away. "You don't want to call nobody. That would be stupid."

She's read the application. That's how she knew where to find me. If I yell for help and someone calls the police, then she'll tell them I steal from old ladies.

She smiles and reaches for the picture frame on top of the TV. "This must be a picture of your daddy. Is this Sylvia?"

I don't answer.

"She's a pretty woman, for her type," Razza says as if we're old friends. "I can see why your daddy, he would fall for her."

"Sylvia has come back. She's at work now, but she'll be home soon."

"Oh? You know, I'd love to meet her." Razza unbuttons her coat, making herself comfortable.

"You can't stay."

Razza just smiles.

"She got nothing in there," Sasa says, coming out of Sylvia's room. "I'm going to see if she has something good to eat."

Razza says something in a language I can't understand. It sounds rough, the words come from low in her throat.

Sasa drops down on the couch, looking like she wants to throw a tantrum. But she spots the cookies and grabs up the bag instead.

"We have to talk, Casey," Razza says, settling herself at the table. "I've been thinking I would benefit from a nicer place to do business from, you know?"

"I thought you did business through the mail."

"Some, this is true. Not all. There are always seekers who want more guidance, who are not satisfied to read from ancient writings. They want the personal touch. Like yourself."

Real fear moves deep in my belly. I don't care if Razza takes something from the apartment. If I had any money left, I'd give it to her. But Razza wants the apartment.

I hear the distant boom of the incinerator slamming shut in the basement. Paulie's cleaning up down there. "Close the door, Casey," Razza says.

I run across the hall, throw open the heavy door to the incinerator closet, and yank the chute open. "Paulie! Paulie! Paul—" Sasa grabs me by the collar, yanks me back into the corridor, and the door slams shut. She reaches back with one arm to slap me, but Razza stops her.

Down the hall, old Mrs. Wisner opens her door. "Casey, is something the matter?" She takes one look at Razza, and with the slightest movement to suggest she's about to close her door, she says, "I'm calling the police."

"That is not necessary," Razza says. "I'm Sylvia's tarot reader. I came to read for her and I find she is not at home."

"They're just going," I hear myself say. "Right this minute." I look hard at Razza. Reminding her she has as much to lose as I do.

"Stop playing with Sylvia's little girl, Sasa," Razza says. "We have another appointment." She walks slowly to the elevator, a slow walk that reminds me of kids on the playground. Kids looking for trouble.

Sasa follows her into the elevator. Razza never even looks back. When they're gone, Mrs. Wisner says, "Is Sylvia coming home soon?"

"Soon," I say, like it's a promise.

"Why don't you come over?" Mrs. Wisner says.

"No, thanks. I have homework."

She says, "You can stay with me until Sylvia comes home. I'll make up the cot."

"I'll be okay. I won't open the door again."

"All right, then," Mrs. Wisner says.

It isn't until I'm back in the apartment that Mrs. Wisner's words sink in, really sink in. *I'll make up the cot.* Mrs. Wisner knows I'm staying here alone. It gives me the shakes to think about it. Paulie, Razza, now Mrs. Wisner, who else knows?

I'm about to turn on the TV for company when I hear the elevator stop at my floor. It doesn't matter that I'm almost expecting it. When the doorbell rings, it makes me jump.

TWENTY-EIGHT

I'm ready, though. Not loud or anything, just definite. "Go away."

"It's me. Paulie."

My fingers are shaking so much, the chain takes forever to come free. I'm so relieved to see him. It's even funny that Mrs. Wisner opens her door at the same time. Paulie and I look down the hall at her, there's this big grin on my face.

Mrs. Wisner nods. "Your father has you looking in on her," she says. "That's good."

"Yes, ma'am," Paulie says. Son of the super. Mrs. Wisner shuts her door.

"What's going on?" he asks when he comes into the apartment.

"Did you hear me call for you? Down the incinerator shaft?"

"The whole building heard you," he says. "I see you haven't been arrested."

Of course that's what he would think of. It never occurred to me.

"It's not something like you let the bathtub run over, is it?" he asks, glancing around the room for signs of a disaster.

I tell him all of it, expecting him to get mad that I went to Razza's apartment. He sits down on the couch and hears me out about second chances. He interrupts only once, to ask, "Did you check around? They didn't take your keys or anything?"

"No," I say, patting my pocket. I never leave my keys lying around anymore. I'm afraid of getting locked out.

When it's all told, he asks, "You aren't going to work with me again, are you?"

I can tell I've hurt him somehow. It's so hard to say no to Paulie. I still need him, and not just because he can sign checks.

"Well, hey, that's all right," he says. "There's no place in this business for somebody with scruples."

I don't know how he does it, he makes me laugh.

He orders Chinese takeout, then offers to help me with my homework. "You're worse than Sylvia. All the time you spend thinking about homework, somebody'd think you were an A student."

"I am an A student," he says. "Anybody who skips as much school as I do can't afford to fall down on the work, else I'd still be back in fifth grade. Besides, I like studying. I like to get A's."

"Oh."

My homework, on the other hand, is worse than ever. I owe Mrs. Blume two assignments. Plus some homework from before the Tuesday I missed. And a report Mrs. Lesky assigned right after Sylvia left was due Friday. I don't like to owe homework any more than I like to do it.

I say, "Well, as long as you're really going to help."

Karen calls while we're working. It's a strange call, but it's not her fault. She expects me to be glad she called, and I am, sort of. But it's like she's somebody I knew a long time ago.

She tells me about some television show we both used to watch. I haven't seen it since Sylvia left. Paulie's making a wind-it-up sign at me, I can't tell Karen he's there. We have nothing to talk about.

"I have to go," I say to her. "It was nice of you to call."

She hangs up. No good-bye. Just hangs up.

"Okay," I say, so he shouldn't get the idea he's the boss of me now. "Who went to war with who while I was on the phone?" I sound just like Sylvia.

"It's not a good time to chat," he says. "You don't see me hanging on the street corner, do you? It's too easy to let something slip."

He's right. I know he's right. So I let it drop.

Paulie takes his empty food containers to the kitchen, he spots the dead mouse under the napkin. He doesn't kid me about it. He just walks to the bathroom, holds the trap over the toilet and flushes the mouse down.

Paulie stays until nearly eleven. "You afraid they'll come back?" he asks.

I shake my head. Razza might come back. But I'm not opening the door again without looking outside first.

"Put the chain on," he says. "Turn on the TV if the quiet gets to you."

The only thing left to do is watch movies. Then I get this crazy idea to call Fran. I can't tell her about Sylvia. But what if Sylvia's there? She might go there with Jim so Fran could meet him.

I make a frantic search for Sylvia's phone book, the place is such a mess. Fran's number is written on the line for the fire department.

And then I dial.

While the phone is ringing, I wonder whether this is the right thing to do. I push the thought away. I have to know if Sylvia is there.

Fran answers. Her voice is so much like Sylvia's, but hoarse, too, like she goes over it with a nail file. Hot tears spring to my eyes. My voice comes out like it belongs in a cartoon when I say, "May I speak to Sylvia, please?"

"To Sylvia? My Sylvia? Who is this?"

I hang up, my hands shaking so hard, I fumble the phone.

If I was Paulie, I'd have thought of a good reason to call. I'd have called after school to ask about something normal, like did she think it was okay for me to use the oven to make slice-and-bake cookies. And Fran would have told me if Sylvia had been there, I know she would.

I messed up.

Fran sounded like she might have been sleeping. Maybe she'll go right back to sleep, and in the morning, she'll think it was a dream.

I'm still shaking. I shuffle my books and papers around. Stare at them without really knowing which is which. When the telephone rings a few minutes later, I jump like I got a shock.

There's a good chance it's Fran calling. Not that she could be sure that was my voice, especially the way it squeaked out. Three rings. . . .

It's too bad we don't have an answering machine so I'd know for sure if it was her. Five rings. No more.

Maybe it wasn't Fran.

I make microwave popcorn and chew my way through a movie. I can't keep my mind on the story. The call, the sound of Fran's voice, made me jittery. I'm still in front of the TV at 12:30. I turn the TV off. It's sort of a test to see whether I can stand the quiet.

The elevator stops at my floor, somebody's coming home late. I listen for footsteps.

I don't hear anything.

Until the doorbell rings.

TWENTY-NINE

The stool is by the door. If Razza doesn't give up and go away, I can beat on the door with that little wooden stool. Make so much noise, the entire floor will turn out into the corridor. Razza won't want that kind of attention. I creep to the door and pick up the stool. And wait.

A terrible silence follows.

I drop to a squat and set the stool down very quietly. I can look under the door to see if somebody's shoes block the light from the hallway.

Somebody knocks three times.

I fall away from the door, goose bumps springing up all over my arms and legs. Backed up against the couch, my breath is coming fast. My heart's beating loud enough to hear it like a drumbeat.

I stare hard at the door. The knocks came at the bottom, where nobody would knock. Unless they could see me and know that's right where I was.

They knock again, still real low on the door. And softly.

And then, a voice comes through. Like it's right on the floor. "It's me. Paulie."

I run to the door. It's him, of course it's him, but it's late, so late, and there's this business of knocking, he gave me a scare. "How do I know for sure?"

After a long moment, he says, "I wanna come to the party."

I slide the chain off, open the door. He's on the floor.

Good thing he told me he's Paulie, because I have to look twice to be sure. He has bruises and a black eye, one cheek is swollen like he has a wad of gum in there, his lip is cut. I drop to my knees beside him.

"Ain't you going to ask me in?" he says.

"Paulie, what happened to you?"

"Hey, this ain't a place to talk," he says, rolling away from me onto his side. "Help me inside."

He pushes himself up on one arm and I reach for the other. "Ah! Not that one," he says, making me realize he's been holding it close to his chest in a funny way. "Let me lean on you." He throws his good arm over my shoulder and we stand together. Paulie can use only one leg to bear his weight. He's pretty heavy.

The door to the next apartment opens. We can't get inside before the neighbor guy steps out with a bag of garbage. He stops midstep. Behind him, real low, I can hear the music that goes with the *thump, thump* I usually hear through the wall.

I don't even look at him, as if I can pretend he isn't there. I have such a strong sense that everything in me is about to break.

THIRTY

After a breathless space, the neighbor says, "Everything okay out here?"

I nod. Paulie kind of hops into the apartment, putting his sore foot down for only a moment so that I don't have to really carry him. With his arm over my shoulder he sort of pulls me along.

Once we're inside, he swings around to put his hand against the wall. "Lock the door," he says. He's on one leg, his hand on his chest like a Boy Scout making a promise.

"What happened?" He looks like a bad dream. "Paulie?"

"Let me sit."

We get him over to the couch. "That guy going to call anybody?" he asks as we shuffle along.

"I don't think so," I say. "Sylvia always called him a guy who minds his own business."

"I'm gonna need some ice on this foot," he says as he eases it onto the coffee table. "You got ice?"

"I think so."

"Otherwise, maybe you could borrow from the neighbor," he says, making a joke.

"I got ice. What happened to you?"

"Loach," Paulie says, making the name sound like a disease.

"He beat you up like this?" Like I don't already know.

"Aw, I don't care," he says. "Hey, you got that ice?"

The ice tray is stuck. I get the hammer Sylvia keeps in the hardware drawer to knock it out of the freezer. Fold a dish towel for an ice bag. It's like I take care of these problems every day.

He's prying off his sneaker. I sit down on the coffee table. "Want me to pull?"

"No," he says. "Well, yeah. It hurts, okay?"

I get my fingers in at the sides of the sneaker and yank at the shoe. I think it will be a fast, painless method. It isn't painless, it isn't fast, either. Even when he yowls and clings to the back of the couch, I keep on pulling. The shoe pops off.

His foot is fat, colored red and purple. He stares at it for a moment, then looks at me kind of sheepishly. "He stomped on it."

"He stomped all over you?"

He sets his foot down on the table and puts the ice pack on his foot. Right away the ice slides out the sides of the folded towel.

"Just get it to stay on top or something," he says. Then falls back like he's exhausted. I stack magazines at each side of his foot to support the ice. That works.

"How about your arm?" I ask.

"It got twisted a little. It'll be fine in a couple of days."

"Your face?"

"Just let me rest a minute. You'd be amazed what hard work it can be to get around when all your parts aren't working right."

"Why did he do this?"

"He found the money. Our money."

"So he knows it's stolen?"

"He got mad because I'm holding out on him," he says with a lift of his eyebrows.

I know Paulie's life is way worse than mine, even with Sylvia running out on me. I just had no idea how bad that meant. Whatever Sylvia did, I knew she always meant well.

Even now, wherever she and the boyfriend are, Sylvia's probably hoping for the best for both of us. I hate Sylvia. But I also wish she was here.

"Here's the thing. You don't have to worry, because he didn't get it all. He didn't get even half."

"I don't care about—"

"You gotta care. There's enough money to get us outta this city. We can go away someplace—"

"Go away where, Paulie?" I yell. "We're kids!"

He looks at me like maybe he's coming up with an argument.

"You promised your mother you'd go to school," I say. "And I'm waiting here for Sylvia."

He tries to stare me down. I won't give in. "For a little girl," he says finally, "you got grit."

"We're fine here," I say shakily. "We'll think of something."

"Yeah. He just needs time to cool off. You don't care if I stay here a couple of days, right?"

"You don't have to go back." I try to look past his bruised and swollen face to see the Paulie I know is still in there. "We'll think of something better than that."

"It's the Loaches or it's somebody like them. Maybe somebody worse."

"Maybe somebody better."

"Now look at that," he says. "You didn't strike me as the type to believe in fairy tales."

"Sometimes I do. Sometimes."

"You got something to eat?" he says as if the subject has worn him out. "Something soft?"

"Like soup?"

"Too runny."

I have a couple of cans of Chef Boyardee. "Ravioli?"

"Sounds good."

When I bring him the food, he has to gather his strength to eat. "You got nothing to do?" he asks. I get it. He's embarrassed.

Looking around, it's like I'm seeing the apartment for the first time in days. Dishes are on every table and on top of the

TV. I spend a few minutes hanging up some clothing I left in the living room and then pick up dishes.

"Hey, you don't have to go into this cleaning frenzy because I'm company or something," Paulie says. He's finished all but a couple of ravioli.

"I just feel like it."

"We have to talk about the money, so could you sit down?"

"You mean there's some left?"

"Sure. I got it hidden in the laundry room. You're going to have to go get it now."

THIRTY-ONE

"Me?" I don't like the sound of this.

"He's going to start thinking. About whether there might be more money stashed somewhere. And then he's going to go looking."

"Where was the money he found? In your room?"

"In a storage closet," he says. "Behind a panel that used to be for the dumbwaiter. Most of the shaft is still there, just it's closed off everywhere except in this closet."

"So what makes you think he'll look in the laundry room?"

"It's the same kind of hiding place. He knows the nooks and crannies in this building as well as I do. He's been super here since before we were born. Sooner or later, he'll come to the one in the laundry room."

"Isn't the laundry room locked now?"

He opens his hand to show me. The key.

My heart sinks.

He says, "He's probably asleep."

He has a plan, of course. I should go down the stairs. Quietly. In the basement, I should check that the service entrance is locked before going into the laundry room. That means Mr. Loach has made his rounds. It's good Paulie has a plan. I'm doing as little thinking as possible.

As I'm going out the door, Paulie says, "Casey, wait."

I look back at him.

"If he finds you, yell. Yell like you did before. The vents in that room carry sound all through the building, just like the incinerator shaft. Yell until somebody shows up, okay?"

He's scaring me. I go fast, while I still can.

In the basement, the service entrance is locked. I go back and unlock the laundry room and turn on the lights. I let the door shut behind me. That's the one thing I do different. Paulie said to leave it open so I can hear the elevator if it comes.

What good is it to hear the elevator? It's better if the laundry room door is shut. Unless someone is coming here anyway, they won't notice it isn't locked. I find the place behind the last two washing machines that Paulie told me about.

The machines are on a block that isn't solid, it's cement laid over a heavy wood frame. The cement broke off at one corner. Paulie's chipped away at the hole until he could shove in a smallish paper bag stuffed with money. He put two bags in there, he said.

It didn't bother me, the idea of reaching in for them, until Paulie told me not to worry about rats. That they scare easier than people think. So I brought my twelve-inch ruler, figuring I'd put that in first, test to see if anything pounces on it.

Nothing does.

When I pull the bags out and stand up, the laundry room door opens.

THIRTY-TWO

A little scream escapes me. But it's only Mrs. Gonzales.

"Casey, *querida,* what you doing down here so late? I thought I was the only night owl in the building."

My mind is a blank.

"*Querida!* Your hair! That short cut is just darling on you!" Mrs. Gonzales runs her hands over my hair. "Where did you get it done?"

"The barber." I tuck the bags under one arm like library books. The bags make that kind of package, like Paulie must have stacked the bills neatly and tied them together. That's the way he does things.

"The barber! Did Sylvia think of this? What a change for you! Do you love it or do you *love* it?"

"I love it."

Mrs. Gonzales fusses over me, then tells me she left two loads of laundry down here. "I'm reading in bed, thinking it's time to turn out the light, when I remember! I'm gonna be lucky if it's still here."

It is. "My mind, I don't know where I keep it," she says, giving herself a little knock on the head before she takes the stuff out of the dryers. "I waited and waited for the towels to dry, and finally it's nearly dinnertime and I says to myself,

Gigi, if you don't go up and stir the meatballs, they're gonna stick." She pulls out a wad of towels and puts them in my arms, talking all the time. "Out of sight, out of mind!"

Mr. Loach appears in the doorway. I tighten my arm against the money. "How'd you two get in here?" he says in an ugly way.

Mrs. Gonzales isn't at all put off. She's shaking out a pair of jeans as she says, "The door was open, so we came in. A good thing, too, because I had laundry left down here and I wouldn't be too shy to knock on your door in the middle of the night." I'm carefully making sure Paulie's bags are hidden by the towels.

"This room was locked at nine o'clock," Mr. Loach says.

"Oh, now, don't you worry," Mrs. Gonzales says. "We aren't going to report you to the management. We're happy I can get my laundry, aren't we, Casey?"

"Sure." My tone of voice is as good as a shrug. I follow Mrs. Gonzales out, both of us up to our ears in laundry. It's crazy, what I'm thinking. She must take a lot of showers to need so many towels.

Mr. Loach just stands there as we get on the elevator.

Mrs. Gonzales talks all the way to her apartment. We drop the laundry onto a chair. "You want a little something? I got a guava nectar in the fridge."

"No, thanks," I say, adjusting the bags under my arm. "Sylvia will wonder why I'm taking so long."

I figure I made a clean getaway.

THIRTY-THREE

"Where's your ruler?" Paulie asks, first thing after I show him the bags.

I hate to admit it. "I left it there."

He doesn't say anything. It's hard to say which is worse, the Paulie before or this one, who expects everything to go wrong.

"I can go back down for it."

"Nah. If he didn't see you, there's no reason for him to connect the ruler to you."

"He saw me." I tell him about meeting Mrs. Gonzales in the laundry room.

"He didn't see you standing where you left the ruler?"

"Nope."

"Okay. Let's forget about it."

"Are you sure?"

"I don't want to chance him finding you there a second time," he says.

"What do we do with this?" I ask, reminding him about the money.

"Stick it in the broiler."

While I'm doing that, he yells, "Not too far in. We don't want the pilot light to set it on fire."

Which gets me thinking again, about how different Paulie's life has been from mine. I go back to the living room, asking, "Why do you stay with him if you could go somewhere else?"

He shrugs. "Some fosters, they're all over you like cat fur. Loach, he let me do what I needed to do. Turned a blind eye, you know? So long as he had something to gain."

"So, what happened?"

"My mistake. Just because he's too stupid to look for something doesn't mean he can't get lucky and stumble over it." He offers another embarrassed shrug. "Everybody makes mistakes sometimes, right?"

I hope so. I'd hate to be the only one.

Paulie's shifted around to lie on the couch, like he plans to sleep there. I'm real quiet at first, trying not to clink the glasses I pick up. And then less so. It doesn't seem to matter. He falls asleep anyway.

My dad said once that everybody has some part that hasn't grown up. That maybe never grows up. In Paulie, that part only shows itself when he sleeps. With the bruised side of his face turned away, he looks sweet somehow.

He doesn't like to be stared at, though, so I won't stare. I drop an afghan over him and go on cleaning up. When I finish, I turn on the TV. I keep it low, worried that it'll wake Paulie. But he's dead to the world.

▪ ▪ ▪

The TV's still on when Paulie wakes me. "Hey, it's time you got ready to go to school."

"School?" Somehow, I'd lost track of the fact that Monday morning would follow Sunday.

"You can't miss another day."

Paulie looks awful. Either his face is worse or I'd forgotten how bad it was. I put my head in my hands. "I feel dizzy."

"I don't care if you got bubonic plague. You missed last Tuesday. You go to school every day this week."

"What about you? Don't you have to go to school?"

His face slides into that street-tough look he has, even all beaten up the way he is, and his voice matches. "They used to me not showing up." He looks like a bad imitation of himself.

"Well, nobody will think I played hooky if I miss today."

"Maybe you'll feel better if you have something to eat," he says. He's weakening.

"I don't think so."

After a minute he says, "You ever feel like this before? What does Sylvia do when you don't feel good?"

"Sylvia never knows exactly what to do when I get sick. She calls the doctor and he reminds her. 'Give Casey this medicine, feed her toast and ginger ale until her stomach settles, and don't let her go back to school until the fever is gone for three days.' "

"You think you got a fever?" It's the first time I've heard Paulie sounding like he might not know what to do. "Only thing worse than not going to school is having to come back home. We don't want the school calling Sylvia to come pick you up."

He's managed to get his hurt arm pulled back inside his sweatshirt so that his elbow kind of rests in the sleeve. It's like a sling for a broken arm. He sees me looking.

"It's okay. I can relax better if I have a little support for it. Now, you really think you're too sick to go in?"

"I'm okay. Sylvia says I'm just a slow starter."

I go off to shower. Before the haircut, a shower would have made me late to school. Now my hair combs easily, dries fast. I can hear the next-door neighbor's radio. *Thump, thump, thump, thump, thump.* Right on schedule.

Paulie calls through the door. "Can I fix you some breakfast?"

"I think you ought to stay where you are," I say, opening the bathroom door. "On the couch."

He limps back to the couch looking lumpy and bent, like the mouse he flushed down the toilet. I make breakfast for both of us. Just dry cereal.

"I can't eat this yet," he says, giving the bowl a little shake. "Got to let it get mushy."

"Well, then, I better get you some milk." I go back to the kitchen.

One of those yogurt drinks Sylvia bought is still in the fridge. They're supposed to be healthy. I shake it up, open it and sniff. On a thought, I put a teaspoon of sugar in it, cap it and shake it again. That's what I give Paulie.

"These are disgusting."

I agree, but I say, "I added sugar. You'll live through it."

He finishes the whole thing. "Wasn't so disgusting as I thought," he says.

The street voice has dropped away again. He sounds like anybody else. The anybody else I like best. I know better than to say that.

He adds, "I just figured they were cheesy or something."

"Live and learn," I say in that crisp way Sylvia did when I had been stubborn and then changed my mind.

"All right, all right," he says.

The phone rings.

"Don't answer it," he says as I reach for it.

"Why not?" It rings again.

"I got a bad feeling," he says. "What if he knows I'm here?"

THIRTY-FOUR

"How could he know?" The phone's still ringing.

He shrugs. "The ruler, maybe. Anybody who calls you this time of day?"

"No." It's not even eight o'clock.

"Why don't you have an answering machine?" he asks in an annoyed way.

"It stopped working right." Besides, it hardly ever had messages we cared about anyway. "Sylvia was home most of the day. Me in the evening."

When the phone goes on ringing for so long, I begin to think Sylvia might call before I go to school. "It might be Sylvia."

"She hasn't called yet, what makes you think she's calling this particular morning?" Paulie says.

"I don't know. Who rings this long unless it's an emergency?"

"Loach. In his mind, this is an emergency."

It rings another three times and quits.

There's only one question in my mind. "If he knows you're here, wouldn't he just come up?"

"If he *thinks* I'm here, he'll check it out."

"Will you be safe here while I'm at school?"

"He has a key."

"To this apartment?" I go immediately to the door and put on the chain.

"That won't do it," Paulie says. "After you go, I'll push the couch up against it."

"I'm not going anywhere."

Paulie doesn't argue. "Give me a hand with the couch, will you?"

Mr. Loach doesn't come up. The phone rings off and on all morning. Every twenty minutes to half an hour. Like someone means to drive us crazy.

It drives us crazy.

We bicker all morning about whether or not I should pick up, whether or not we should unplug the phone. We can't agree. Sometimes we turn on the TV, sometimes we turn it off. And then everything gets quiet. Even the street is quiet. At first it feels good. Then it goes on too long.

"How come old movies?" I ask. "What do you like about them?"

"Happy endings, mostly. They're more believable in old movies."

This is not the kind of answer I expected.

"Everybody gets their happy endings somewhere," he adds. "Hey, you got any macaroni and cheese?"

I do. I got some of the frozen kind at the store, mainly because Sylvia didn't ever get it. She said it wasn't as good as making it herself. She was right. I fix it and sit with him while he eats. His bad foot is propped up on the coffee table and he has long, smooth toes, even though two are kind of swollen.

Sylvia had this theory about people, that they like to be with people whose toes match their own. Some people have long toes they can use to pick up pencils off the floor. Some people have knobby toes that look like the beginnings of tree roots.

Our family, Sylvia said, has short, round toes. Mine are short and round, Sylvia's are short and round, my dad's were short and round. Probably my mom's were, too. It always made me feel especially good that Sylvia included my mom. Now I like knowing my toes match Sylvia's.

The phone starts in again.

I say, "If that's Sylvia and she doesn't come home, I'll never forgive you." I don't think it's Sylvia anymore. Sylvia would think I was in school at this time of day. It just seems like a good thing to say. It's my phone, after all. "If it turned out to be him, can't I just say I'm home with the flu? He wouldn't come busting in here then, would he?"

Paulie shrugs.

Just when I reach to pick the phone up, it stops. Twenty minutes pass. Half an hour. An hour more. Silence.

It's almost worse.

Paulie says, "I don't think it was him."

"Good."

"It wasn't her, either."

"I know."

He looks up a little sheepishly. "You sure?"

"Yeah."

"Still think you're gonna hear from her, huh?"

"Maybe."

A few minutes pass during which we don't say anything. I know Paulie won't leave it alone. He's Paulie.

"She doesn't deserve you," he says.

"She was real nice to me when I was little. The other girlfriends my dad had were only nice to me if he was around where he could hear. And Sylvia took good care of me after he died. She didn't have to, you know."

I can almost hear what he's thinking. Yeah, well, she's not taking good care of you now. It's nice of him not to say it.

"Got anything in that kitchen besides macaroni and cheese?"

I'm getting hungry, too, so I make up some of Sylvia's potato soup. Put boxes of frozen potatoes in cheese sauce and frozen chopped broccoli in cheese sauce in a glass bowl and into the microwave until the potatoes defrost. Chop up a frozen breakfast sausage. Open a can of Campbell's mushroom soup. When the potatoes and broccoli are ready, I spoon the soup over them, add milk and the sausage and stir. Pop the whole deal back in for another few minutes.

When I check, it's done, except it needs another little stir.

"Wow," Paulie says after the first spoonful of thick soup. "This is pretty good."

"It's Sylvia's recipe."

We eat in silence. We're still sort of waiting for the phone to ring. When we finish, Paulie asks, "What makes you think she'll come back?"

"She has to, that's all."

Paulie thinks this over. "It happens every day that happy endings don't come," he says.

"I know Sylvia," I say irritably.

When I get up to take our bowls to the kitchen, he grabs my wrist. "Maybe you're right, then," he says. "She'll come back."

"You don't believe that."

"I don't believe in a lot of things," he says with a shrug. "That don't make them impossible."

That Paulie.

THIRTY-FIVE

It's a little after three when the doorbell rings. We'd turned off the television just seconds before, so we didn't even have the sound from the elevator to warn us. We both jump about a mile.

Paulie puts a finger to his lips. The doorbell rings again. I stand up, I can't sit still.

We wait.

Somebody puts a key into the lock.

I scream, "Who is it?"

Paulie, meanwhile, is up and hop-stepping toward the nearest doorway, which leads to my room. I'm right behind him. He stops at the door.

"Is there somebody in there?" Mr. Loach calls with this fake niceness in his voice. "Is that you, uh, honey?"

"Don't let on you know it's him yet," Paulie whispers to me. "Ask, who is it."

"Who is it?"

"It's me, the super. I have to come in to check the ceiling," he says. "Somebody upstairs has a leak."

"That's a trick," Paulie whispers. "Everybody opens the door for the super when he says that."

Getting closer to the door, I tell him, "I'm home sick. Sylvia said not to open the door until she comes home."

"That's for strangers, honey. This is me, the super."

"Sorry. Sylvia told me."

He unlocks the door. The couch keeps it from opening. "You better quit that," I yell. I'm not pretending. "I'm going to tell Sylvia on you. I'm going to call the police, too, because she always says to."

"Hey now, don't go getting upset," Mr. Loach calls in. Further away, Mrs. Wisner asks him what's going on. I'm beginning to like Mrs. Wisner a lot.

Mr. Loach answers her with the same story about a leak. I reach over and press on the door until the lock catches. A couple of seconds later, Mrs. Wisner calls in to me, "Casey, dear, I'll stay with you while Mr. Loach checks the ceilings."

Arrrgh. Mrs. Wisner.

"I checked," I call back. "They're fine. I'm sick, Mrs. Wisner. And I'm supposed to be in bed."

Mr. Loach says something that sounds rude. Mrs. Wisner says something that sounds like she's trying to reason with him. It's terrible to make Mrs. Wisner face him alone.

I look at Paulie, who shakes his head no.

"Listen, kid," Mr. Loach yells. Then he pushes on the door again. "What's this? You got something up against the door? What's going on in there?"

With all the noise he's making, I don't hear the elevator. I hear somebody ask what right he has to open this apartment, something like that. I recognize the voice and, getting on the couch, I press my ear to the crack in the door.

"You related to anybody who lives here?" Mr. Loach asks, like this person doesn't have any business asking questions.

"My daughter and her daughter live here." I wave to Paulie to come help me move the couch.

He looks at me like I'm nuts, but he limps over to help. With his good arm he pulls the couch away. I wave him back to the bedroom. I make a motion that means he should shut the door.

Paulie gets behind the door, looks out around the edge.

Mr. Loach has abandoned his story about the ceiling. He's telling Fran that his foster kid ran away from home. That he thinks Paulie is hiding in Sylvia's apartment. I slip the chain off the door and open it just enough to frame my body.

Mrs. Wisner is still there. I notice Fran's carrying two shopping bags from Lord & Taylor, what she calls a "better department store." I know from Sylvia, these are her overnight bags.

Fran looks at me. The look on her face tells me she doesn't like Mr. Loach. Or maybe she just doesn't like the situation she's walked into.

"They all stick together, these kids," Mr. Loach is saying. "Besides, there's nowhere else he could be."

"He has an entire city," Fran says. "What makes you think he's in this apartment?"

"People have seen them together."

Fran lets a silence fall. Her look says she doesn't like him any more than before, but now he's said something that interests her. "How old is the boy in question?" she asks.

"He's sixteen," Mr. Loach says.

"My granddaughter is barely twelve," Fran says. I like that I've gone from being Sylvia's daughter to Fran's granddaughter.

"Kids start bringing home stray dogs when they're a lot younger than that," Mr. Loach says.

Fran uses an arm with a shopping bag hanging from it to push him aside as if she's brushing away flies, and steps past him. "If my granddaughter has already told you your son isn't here, I sincerely doubt that he is."

At the same time, the elevator opens and the neighbor with the loud stereo steps out.

"Hey," he says, "what's going on?"

My heart is beating fast as Fran turns to him and says, "This gentleman seems to think we're hiding his runaway son in our apartment."

She turns to me. "Is he here?"

My face is hot. I can't look at the neighbor as I say, "I told him Paulie wasn't here." She's close enough I can throw my arms around her thick waist. She manages to hug me back with a shopping bag. I say, "Sylvia told me never to let anybody in when she isn't here."

Down the hall, a door opens and another neighbor lady steps out to see what all the fuss is about. "Why should I take a kid's word for it?" Mr. Loach is saying.

"All right then, don't," Fran says. "Take mine. I've been staying here for the last three days and I haven't seen your son." Fran's carrying shopping bags, not a suitcase, so Mr. Loach can't know for sure she's lying to him. That she's just now arriving.

"That's right," Mrs. Wisner chimes in. "Sylvia told me she'd be gone for a couple of days. Casey's grandma has been here keeping an eye on things. I've seen her."

That Mrs. Wisner is full of surprises.

"Yeah, me, too, I seen the grandma here yesterday," the neighbor says. "I know your boy, don't I? He was there when I signed the lease? I saw him last night. He didn't look too good to me, you know anything about that?"

I can look at that neighbor now and I can't help smiling.

Mr. Loach is still angry, but now he also looks confused, like maybe he is making a mistake. Fran chooses that moment to step inside the apartment. I duck inside and lean against the door to shut it. Fran drops her bags onto the couch.

In a low voice, she asks, "Where is he?"

THIRTY·SIX

I point to my room. Fran turns on her heel, and I follow her in.

Paulie sits on the edge of my bed as if he's about to make a run for it. As if he could. Fran doesn't know he can't get much further than back to the couch.

"So you're this Paulie? You're the runaway?"

"If I ran away, I wouldn't still be here," Paulie says. Like he thinks he sounds tough. He looks scared to me, sitting forward with my quilt pulled half over his lap.

"From the looks of you," Fran says quietly, "I have to ask, why didn't you?"

Paulie nods in my direction. "I got friends here."

"Well, the shape you're in, I don't think we have to worry about him calling the police," Fran says. "You can stay a while longer."

Paulie sinks back onto the bed, pulling his sore arm back into his sleeve. Immediately he doesn't look so strong, so capable. He looks like a kid again, the way he did when he slept.

"The real question is," Fran says, "why hasn't someone else called them?"

"He's usually more careful than this," Paulie says. "He lost his temper."

"I'm Sylvia's mother," Fran says. I can see she's deciding to be on Paulie's side. "Fran."

"Can I call you Granny Fran?" he asks.

"A wise guy, yet. So it's just bruises?" Fran asks.

"Except for his foot," I tell her.

"His foot?"

I pull the quilt back a little. "Mr. Loach stomped on it. It's real fat."

"Oh, jeez," Fran says. "You've got to have something broken in there. We can't just leave things like this."

"We're icing it," Paulie says. "Doctors won't set my foot while it's swollen up, anyway."

"This is true," Fran says. "I'd have a doctor come in, but they're going to want pictures."

"Pictures?" Paulie says.

"X rays," I explain. Fran's a dental assistant, they talk like that.

"We'll have to get the swelling down," she says, "and then maybe we can find a doctor."

"We can't leave here," I say. "Mr. Loach might see us."

"It doesn't matter," Fran says. "He knows Paulie is here."

"How does he know?"

"Same way I knew," Fran says. "It's written all over your face."

"Oh." Which pretty much makes it a good thing I decided to go straight, I guess.

"Your neighbors were looking on," she adds. "Mr. Loach didn't want to make more of a scene." As she turns to leave the room, Paulie moves to get up. Fran says, "You stay off that foot."

To me, back in the living room, she says, "I called you this morning."

"How many times?" I ask as I carry her shopping bags into Sylvia's room. Fran just makes a little sound under her breath, so she must've called a lot of times.

I put the bags down just inside the room. Fran packed them like suitcases. She asks, "Where are the clean sheets?"

We put fresh sheets on the bed like it's something we've always done together. And then, like we're talking about somebody we both know but aren't related to, Fran asks, "So what happened exactly? Sylvia made out like she was going for groceries?"

"She went while I was at school."

"Oh. Sure, that would be the way. She took all her clothes?"

"Most." In the kitchen, the broiler opens with a metallic scrape, then shuts. I glance at Fran, and I know she's heard it, too.

Fran goes on shaking a pillow into a pillowcase. "Did Sylvia collect travel brochures? Or learn French or something?"

"No."

"Go out and buy a swimsuit?" I just look at Fran, who asks, "Did she say anything that might have been a hint of some kind?"

"A hint?"

"Like, she always wanted to live in California?"

"She said, 'If I ever get married again.' That worried me."

"Really."

"Whoever she marries is going to be the boss of us."

Fran stares at me a moment, then says, "Good point."

Fran motions for me to pass her another pillow. "I feel like a good cup of joe, how about you?"

Fran's word for coffee. "Sure," I say, even though I don't like it. Paulie is settled in the living room now, and he turns on the TV, keeping the sound low.

In the kitchen, Fran takes a look at what she calls the larder. She means she's checking for what there is to eat. She quickly looks through the fridge, into the freezer.

She doesn't look into the broiler or ask me about it.

When she tastes the soup I left in the pot, I say, "It's Sylvia's recipe."

"Good," she says. "It's important to eat right." Fran does let me have coffee. A very little bit. She puts a lot of milk in it and plenty of sugar. I still don't like it, but she's tried so hard I'd rather not tell her so.

She's made a cup of coffee for Paulie, also mostly milk. He takes one sip, looks at me, then at Fran, who's not waiting for his reaction. She's on her way back to the dining room table. He says, "Thanks for the milk shake."

"Wisenheimer," Fran says. She's wearing a quirky little smile, though, when she sits down across from me.

"That's like 'you're welcome' in some foreign language, right?" Paulie says to her.

Fran answers him. "That's right."

She takes a piece of paper from my notebook and makes a shopping list. She has me look in the cabinets and tell her what's there. When Fran asks me what I like to eat, she asks Paulie, too. I like that. In between the items she puts on the list, she asks about other things. "Why didn't you tell somebody? If not me, a neighbor. Or a teacher."

"I didn't want Sylvia to get in trouble over this," I say, sitting back down. "They might take me away from her when she comes back."

"I don't think so," Fran says. "Mostly they try to keep mothers and children together."

"I'm not really her child."

"You are. Sylvia adopted you right after she married your father."

"You know what I mean. Mothers get in trouble for leaving their children, it could be worse for a stepmother." We're quiet then, staring into our coffee.

After a few minutes Fran says, "I feel like this is my fault. Mostly my fault, anyway."

"How could it be your fault?" I thought it was my fault, it hadn't occurred to me that Fran might feel the same way.

She jots something down. "There's something you have to understand about Sylvia," she says. "She needs someone to lean on. Maybe we all need that, but my Sylvia needs it more." Fran puts a few more things on her list.

"Is that why you think she left?"

She glances up. "Don't you? I hope you don't think you disappointed her somehow, do you?"

I don't say anything.

"Because Sylvia loves you very much," Fran says.

I can hardly stand to hear this. I take a swallow of the coffee to relieve the sudden cramp in my throat.

"Sylvia's trouble is," Fran says, "she thinks happiness is something that lasts and lasts, like silverware."

"Doesn't happiness last?"

"Oh, it does. But it isn't always shiny. It can lose a little gloss. And sometimes we get so caught up in worry or hard times that we think we've lost it."

"Maybe we do lose it."

"It sparkles," Fran says with greater conviction. "It's there for a moment when the light catches it, and then you have to wait for the light again." Her eyes kind of squeeze the idea, so I know she really believes. She adds, "It's worth the wait."

I look at Fran, seeing her differently than I have before. "You know, you sound like Sylvia's mom."

"I'm going to take that as a compliment," she says.

THIRTY-SEVEN

Fran calls her order in to the supermarket, then says, "It's getting late. We should have something to eat now."

"We could order pizza," I suggest.

"Not a chance," Fran says. "What we need is real food."

"Oh, no," Paulie groans. "Not nutrition."

Fran makes fried egg sandwiches. Over dinner, I tell her about keeping my secret at school, especially from Karen. About thinking I saw Sylvia on the street. When we're doing the dishes, I tell Fran about Mrs. Clark. I don't say it was Paulie's idea. I don't have to.

I thought it would be much harder to tell her about Mrs. Clark than it is. Fran has a way of making me feel that everything I did was just what anybody would have done if they were in my place. Only Sylvia has ever done that for me before, like when I threw away the first report card I ever got with an F on it.

The part that upsets Fran most is the way Razza came into the apartment. "You've been through so much these last two weeks," she says.

"She's got grit," Paulie says from the couch.

"You yourself are not in short supply," Fran says, and

makes Paulie laugh. It's funny how he and Fran sort of like each other.

"Tell me about this car you drive around in," Fran says. "Where'd you get it?"

"It belongs to Loach. He doesn't like to bother with moving it from one parking space to another, that's my job," Paulie says. "I got a learner's permit now, which is more than I had when I was driving two years ago."

"So there's an improvement," Fran says. "He doesn't *know* or doesn't *care* that you do more than find parking spaces?"

"Doesn't care," Paulie says. "He can always claim he didn't know, if I get into trouble."

When someone knocks on the door about half an hour later, Fran and I are doing the dishes. Fran turns off the water. "Could it be the market already?" she asks in a low voice.

Fran calls out, "Who is it?" as we leave the kitchen.

There's no answer. Fran motions Paulie to hide in the bedroom again and I look out the peephole, half expecting to see Mr. Loach.

It's two men. One in a suit, one in a sweatshirt.

The one in a suit holds a badge up in front of the peephole. I stagger when I step off my stool, feeling sick, feeling like all that holds me up is the weight in my feet. "It's the police," I whisper as Fran hurries over to me.

I thought Fran was tough. I know Fran is tough, I just had no idea how tough. Fran doesn't hesitate. She opens the door, letting the stool scrape over the floor. "Officers?" she says, like somebody who might even be glad to see them.

"Mrs. Drummond?"

"I'm her mother."

"Is Mrs. Drummond at home?" the one in the suit asks.

"Not at the moment," Fran says. "What's this about?"

The sweatshirt asks, "Mrs. Drummond is acquainted with Mr. James Neuland?"

The boyfriend. Paulie, peeking out from behind my bedroom door, looks so relieved I almost laugh. I feel the same way. Fran asks, "And if she is?"

"Do you think we might come in?" This is the suit.

Paulie moves behind the bedroom door as Fran steps back. The officers introduce themselves, they take seats, one on the couch and one on Sylvia's TV chair, so Fran has to sit at the other end of the couch. I won't let myself look at the bedroom door again. Fran motions to me to sit on the arm of the couch next to her.

The suit says, "Mr. Neuland is being charged with the embezzlement of funds from the company he's worked for."

I don't think Fran is faking it when she looks shocked.

He says, "We thought Mrs. Drummond might know where he would go."

"Where is your daughter?" the sweatshirt asks.

"Sylvia is at my home, supervising a paint job," Fran says. Her tone of voice has changed. She doesn't sound like she's worried that Sylvia's in any trouble. She looks relieved, even. She looks like someone who wants to help the police in any way she can.

I remember what Fran said about Mr. Loach seeing it on my face that Paulie was here. I look at Fran, hoping the look on my face will match hers.

"I have terrible allergies. I can't be in the house with the paint smell," Fran says as she puts an arm around my waist. "So I'm here with Casey, who's sick with a sore throat." Fran's given me the perfect excuse not to say a word.

"Where do you live, Mrs. . . . er. . . ."

"Capotosto," Fran says. "In New Jersey. Why don't I give my daughter a call? You can ask Sylvia anything."

The two policemen glance at each other like they haven't made up their minds. Fran's already reaching for the phone. She punches in her number. And waits. "Sylvia's going to be very upset to hear this," Fran says. "Even though they're pretty much over."

"Over?" the sweatshirt asks.

"As in not really a thing anymore," Fran says. "For maybe a month now." She passes the receiver to the officer. "I'm just getting my machine," she says. "The painters start early, they're gone for the day. Maybe Sylvia stepped out for some fresh air, something to eat."

He passes the receiver back to Fran after listening for a moment. "Where in New Jersey, Mrs. Capotosto?"

"Belmar," she says. "You know the shore?"

"No, ma'am," the suit says. He gets a card out of his wallet as he stands up. "If you would let your daughter know we want to talk with her?"

"I certainly will," Fran says. She stands up, too.

"Did you ever meet Mr. Neuland, Mrs. Capotosto?" the sweatshirt asks as Fran shows them out the door.

"Never had the pleasure," Fran says. "Sylvia was never serious about him."

When Fran shuts the door she says loudly, "Casey, set the oven timer for five minutes. If I don't have something to keep the time, I'll be dialing Sylvia every thirty seconds."

Paulie opens the bedroom door, frankly admiring her. I can just hear him thinking, for an old lady, she's got grit.

Fran walks away from the door, raising her voice enough that it might still be heard in the hallway. "What kind of a man must your mother have been seeing? I'm going to give her a piece of my mind." And takes a deep breath, preparing to go on.

We all hear the elevator stop. Fran drops into Sylvia's chair. She looked tough only moments before. Now she just looks old. "I don't mind telling you that was one of the scariest moments of my life," she says. "Sylvia's funeral flashed before my eyes."

"Sylvia's funeral?" I don't get it. Paulie does.

"You thought they had an accident or something," he says.

"I did," Fran says, and tears wet her eyes. "I thought maybe they found her ID. Maybe they don't know for sure if the body is hers."

I go to Fran. Hug her. Hold on to her. Paulie comes to stand close, then puts a hand on her shoulder. "What do we do now?" I ask.

Fran says, "We wait."

"Wait?"

"And stall. And hope that Sylvia calls soon."

"It's been two weeks already," Paulie says. And then, as if he realizes that isn't so helpful, he asks, "How about if you call the police station and pretend you're Sylvia?"

"Why?" I ask.

"So they'll have the answers to their questions and they won't come back looking for Sylvia," Fran tells me. "It will never work."

"It's a plan." This is Paulie.

"What we have done so far, we have done out of desperation," Fran says. "I've never been able to do something dishonest."

Paulie says, "You lie real well."

Fran isn't even offended. She says, "I always get caught. My luck, they'll want Sylvia to come in."

"They're likely to come back if they don't hear from her soon," Paulie points out.

Fran gives him a sharp look. "Are you able to put any weight on that foot?"

"Sure," he says, and shows her how he can sort of tiptoe on it. It makes him sweat, though.

"So you're good on the big toe," Fran says. "What if I ask you to walk on the outside of your foot?"

He gives her a defeated look. "Can't do it. Not yet, anyway."

"That's where he stepped on you?"

He nods.

She says, "We're going to have to get that foot X-rayed."

"How we going to get out of the building without him seeing me?"

"He's not standing guard at the elevator," Fran says, as if she'll punch him in the nose if he is. "And if he is, do you think he wants to attract attention?"

Paulie and I look at each other. If anybody can do it, Fran can.

THIRTY·EIGHT

Paulie has to go slow. I go to the mail room while they're on their way to the taxi. There are only three envelopes in the box.

It isn't until we're in the taxi that we look at the mail. A book of coupons. An ad. And a real letter. "Heights M-n-g-m-t," I read. "Isn't that the rental people?"

Paulie reaches across Fran and takes the envelope out of my hands. Even faster, she snatches it out of his. She opens the envelope, reads the letter, then laughs a little. " 'Dear Mrs. Drummond,' " she reads. " 'We wish to inform you that you have paid March's rent twice, so you need not send another payment until the May rent is due.' "

Fran looks at me. "Sylvia paid the rent. So you were safe on that front all along."

If I'd known the rent was paid, I wouldn't have robbed the old lady, that's the first thought to come to mind. But I'd have been alone all this time, too. Paulie wouldn't be my friend.

Fran seems to understand this. "Funny how things work out," she says.

Paulie insists on paying for the taxi when we get to the

hospital. He knows right where to go, who to talk to. He has an insurance card in his pocket. "You come prepared," Fran says after a nurse takes the card away to be copied.

"That's me," he says. "Your basic Boy Scout."

We wait for two hours in the emergency room. "Just be grateful this isn't a real emergency," Fran says.

We page through the magazines and read aloud. Fran reads about movies and movie stars, Paulie reads *Fortune.* I'm having a good time, sort of.

That changes when we follow Paulie into a kind of examining room. Three sides of it are curtained off, there are people being examined on each side of us. Paulie gets up on the table. I lean against it, since the only wall has all kinds of oxygen tubes and stuff on it. Fran drags in a chair. We wait without saying one word.

The doctor comes in looking like he's in a hurry. He's nice, though. "You the grandmother, Mrs. Capotosto?" he wants to know.

"I'm a neighbor."

The doctor asks Paulie what happened. Before he can answer, Fran says, "Someone stepped on his foot."

"This bruising is pretty developed," the doctor says.

"It happened last night," Paulie says. "It was only sore then. It got worse overnight."

The doctor's still moving Paulie's toes when he asks, "What's with the arm?"

"Got it caught in a revolving door."

The doctor doesn't react except to say, "Let's have a look."

Fran says, "We'll go outside and wait."

When Paulie's wheeled out half an hour later, he still has his arm under his shirt. Now it has a sling around it made out of an elastic bandage. The doctor says, "Somebody will take you up to X-ray."

A guy in blue clothes rides up in the elevator with us. A different doctor takes over up there. "We should have the X rays in about half an hour," this doctor says. "Why don't you kids go back out to the reception area?"

Paulie hops off the table and back into the wheelchair. I wheel him out. "I'm hungry," I say. "Think they'd mind if we find the cafeteria while we wait?"

"You go ahead," Paulie says. "I'll wait and tell Fran where you went."

"Aren't you starved?"

"Not much."

"It's going to be a while before we get home."

"I ain't going home with you," Paulie says. He's gone back to saying things like "wit chu."

"What do you mean?"

"I mean children's services will show up in a little while and I'll be going with them."

Heat rises to my face. "Fran wouldn't do that."

"Not her," he says. "The doctors. They see this all the time."

My heart begins to beat too fast. "Where can we go?"

"Not we," he says. "You got Granny Fran now."

"Paulie."

"Maybe I'll get a real nice place this time. Doesn't matter. I'm almost old enough to be out of their clutches, anyway."

"Am I going to see you? How will I know where you are?"

"You gonna want to see me?" he asks.

It's too much for me. I press my forehead against his bony shoulder. "Paulie."

"Oh, now don't go turning on the waterworks. I'll call you."

"Really?" I wipe my nose with my sleeve. "You swear?"

"I swear. How many people you think cry to see me go?"

"I'm not crying."

"Yeah, I see that. Don't worry, I'll come visit you and Granny Fran. And Sylvia when she comes back."

"You think Sylvia will really come back?"

"Not a doubt in my mind. She must've had a case of temporary insanity or something. She'll get over it." There's a kind of certainty in Paulie's voice. He's willing, if only for me, to believe in Sylvia.

I want to say thanks and let it go at that. I can't. "How do you know?"

"How do I know? Why, that's what temporary means. Gone today, back tomorrow." He's trying to be funny, I can see that. But I can't laugh, not even to make him happy. "Don't feel bad," he adds. "I liked that we were like a family for a little while."

"Sylvia always told me whatever we want, wants us," I say. "There's sure to be somebody out there who can see you're the kind of boy a family wants."

"See? I knew you believed in fairy tales."

"Oh, Paulie."

"Listen," he says. "I left the old lady's money under your pillow. It's all there."

"We used some of it," I remind him.

"I had more money in the bags," he says impatiently. "I been saving up for a while, you know? In case of an emergency."

"Paulie, I—"

"It's your share," he says as Fran and the doctor come back. I can only make urgent eyes at Paulie as the doctor puts a cast on his foot. Paulie pretends he doesn't see.

I wait impatiently for another minute alone with him. I don't want him to feel like he has to be brave or something. The lady from children's services comes just as the doctor finishes.

"Judy, Judy, Judy," Paulie says when he sees her and makes her smile. It looks like a good beginning.

"Hear things aren't working out for you, Paulie."

"Oh, I don't know," Paulie says. "I got friends." And he introduces me and Granny Fran.

THIRTY-NINE

It's dark outside when we take the subway home from the hospital.

Fran doesn't look any happier with the way things turned out than I am. We don't talk much. As we get up to the street again, somebody taps Fran on the shoulder and says, "I have a question for the little girl, if you wouldn't mind."

My breath catches in my throat. It's the guy with the dog.

"Go ahead," Fran says after peering at him under the streetlight.

He smiles at me. "See here, I've seen you about the neighborhood. I guess you visit someone in my building?"

"Uh-huh."

"You've had a haircut." He sounds like that Australian crocodile guy. "Very nice," he says, smiling some more at Fran. "The thing of it is, I need someone to walk my dog in the afternoon, about the time you get out of school. I thought, since you're there anyway—you are, aren't you? For a reasonable fee, that is. Say, four dollars? For an hour of walking?"

Which means he didn't want to turn me over to the police that day I'd hidden in the mail room. He wanted to give me a job.

"All right, six dollars, then," he says. "Do you think that's enough?"

"Yes. It's enough. But I don't go up there all that often."

"Oh, I see. Well, that's a disappointment."

"I'm sorry." A smile breaks out on my face. "I'd have liked a job."

"Perhaps if you called the school," Fran suggests. "They might recommend someone."

"Fine idea," he says. "I appreciate it. Thank you for your time."

Fran doesn't know what to make of it. "I'm afraid to ask," she says when he's far enough away that he won't hear.

"Don't worry. He's just a guy whose dog wets in elevators." We walk half a block in silence. I'm thinking over what Paulie said. I have Granny Fran.

"Do you want to move in with me?" I ask, and my face goes hot. It's harder to ask than I thought it would be.

"Now that you bring it up," Fran says, "I was wondering if we shouldn't make some plans."

I don't want her to think she has to move in with me. To make up for Sylvia leaving. "I could be a help to you," I point out.

"A help?"

"Not to hurt your feelings, but you're pretty old."

"I'm not," she says indignantly.

"You're older than my dad was."

"I'm not old enough to collect social security for three

years yet," she says. "Besides which, the government is going to move old age up. The way things are going, gray hair will be a sign of middle age only."

"You forget things," I remind her. "You've said so."

"I forget some things," she admits. "I've forgotten those same things my whole life. What I remember, everybody else has forgotten. Like every phone number I ever had. That's a lot. Plus every phone number I need, which is even more. Do you know the numbers for your school, the grocery, the video store?"

"No."

"Well, I do. I read Sylvia's phone book, and I can tell you any number you want. Go ahead."

"The dentist." I can't remember the number, but the end spells teeth, and we're coming to the phone booth on the corner. Fran rattles off the number.

I run ahead to the phone and sure enough, the number ends with 83384. "That's pretty good," I say as Fran reaches the phone booth.

"That was an easy one." After a moment, she says, "Maybe you should come home with me. Until Sylvia comes back."

I can see the dark kitchen window that means Sylvia still has not come home. I can't imagine going on living there without her and now without Paulie. Just thinking about it makes my throat hurt. But I also can't stand to think of Sylvia finally coming home and not finding me there.

"I hope you aren't worried about switching schools and leaving all your friends behind," Fran adds. "Because I want to go home, to my house and my job. I'm too set in my ways to be the one who switches. You got anything against this idea?"

That could work. The house is so big, Fran doesn't use the upstairs anymore. But I only shrug. I can't trust myself not to cry.

"I know it's hard for you to believe somebody could live to get really old," Fran says. "People do it all the time. I'm a healthy woman. I'll live until you're too old to need me."

"What about Sylvia?"

"Sylvia will find us," she says.

In the elevator, a new worry hits me. "Where do you think Paulie is now?"

Fran says, "Sitting in an office somewhere while somebody makes phone calls. There wasn't anything else to do, you know that, don't you?"

I do know. I have a place in my heart for the way I feel right now. A place that knows there are some things we can't do anything about.

We have what Fran calls a light supper, canned tomato soup and toast, then sit down to play Scrabble. We're playing the way Sylvia taught me, like we're making a crossword puzzle together. We can see each other's letters.

Fran has too many r's and e's, an n, a t, and a not very

helpful *v*, so she probably can't win. She tries out a word, *veteran*. "An old soldier," she says. When she spells it out, she doesn't have an *a*.

"Do you remember the kinds of things Sylvia used to say?" I ask as I move my tiles around.

"That dreams are the heartprints of happy travelers," Fran answers. She sounds like Sylvia's just nuts. But she remembers one right off, so I have to laugh.

" 'Wishes are ponies, and fairies will ride,' " I say.

"That Siamese cats' voices are pink," she says. "Fuchsia, to be exact." She shakes her head as if to say, that Sylvia.

" 'Tap your toes and make a wish whenever you wear red shoes—you never know!' "

Fran finally has a Scrabble word, *reverent*.

"Only recently," she says, "have I come to know how hard it is to be an optimist like Sylvia. How much real—as our friend Paulie would say—grit it takes."

My dad used to call Sylvia an unreasonable optimist. And Sylvia would tell him she was not unreasonable. She'd tell him her mother, Fran, grew up worrying an A-bomb would fall on Newark. She was taught to hide under her desk. And when Sylvia was a little girl, Fran took all her pajamas away because she heard fire-retardant pajamas caused cancer in little kids.

With all that is wrong with the world, my dad would say, what makes you feel optimistic?

A-bomb, fire-retardant pajamas, insecticides, fried foods . . . Sylvia would say like she was counting on her fingers, and we're still here.

"You don't think it's stupid to be optimistic?" I ask Fran.

"Certainly not."

I knew that. I always knew that. "Do you think she'll come back?"

"If you had asked me a month ago, would Sylvia run off and leave you, my answer would have been no," Fran says. "I think she'll come back. I believe it."

"Maybe she's called you at home by now," I say, and don't even care that Fran might hear some shakiness in my voice.

She opens her mouth to say something, but before she can, the doorbell rings.

We look at each other, thinking about the police.

"It's probably the lady from down the hall," she says. "We forgot to stop by and tell her how Paulie is doing."

I whisper "Mrs. Wisner" to remind her of the name.

When I open the door, Sylvia is standing there.

FORTY

"Casey, honey," she says in a weak voice.

"Sylvia," Fran cries, and jumps up from the dining room table, sweeping a bunch of Scrabble tiles to the floor.

"Ma." Sylvia's crying. Fran throws her arms around her like she's two years old or something. Sylvia's saying she is sorry, sorry, sorry. Fran's telling her we were so worried about her and everything will be fine now and get hold of yourself.

"You're home now, Sylvia, that's what counts."

"You're just saying that to make me feel better, Ma." Fran finds a box of tissues. Sylvia's still crying and going on about how sorry she is.

I remember how my dad used to make me say exactly what I was sorry about. He said it was the only way he could be sure that I learned my lesson. I think that's how Sylvia should say she's sorry. Everything in me that loves her, that missed her even five minutes ago, has hardened into one huge lump.

I pick up the Scrabble game, carry it to my room, and stay.

I can hear everything.

Sylvia says, "I knew Jim was going, and he wanted me to

go with him. Just me, not Casey. I didn't mean to leave, Ma. I woke up that morning and said to myself, just suppose."

"Suppose what?"

"I thought I was saying, 'Suppose I could be what Casey needs and Jim would be what I need and Casey might even turn out to be what Jim needs. We could be happy.' " Sylvia laughs a little. "I just had to convince Jim and Casey."

"Oh, Sylvia," I hear Fran sigh.

"Did you see how she looked at me?" Sylvia says, and I know she means me. "She hates me."

"She doesn't hate you," Fran says. "Did you ever hate me?"

"Sometimes."

"It wasn't hate."

Sylvia manages a little laugh. "No. But it seemed like it at the time."

"You're pale. How long since you ate something?" Fran asks.

"Just coffee since last night."

"You go talk to her," Fran says. "Then you and I have something else to talk about. I'll make eggs and toast."

Sylvia sits down on the bed, close to me. I won't even look at her. "I like your hair."

Right. Like she was gone and I went straight out to get my hair cut. Sylvia doesn't know why I did it, though, and she adds, "It's very chic."

And then, "I know you're awake."

I ask, "Why'd you come back?"

"I missed you."

Two voices. Almost nothing gets past Sylvia. It's the best and the worst thing about her. Because the next thing she says is, "I'm sure you missed me, too, so don't even try to pretend."

I don't answer.

"I know you're mad. You should be."

I know how much easier it was for me to tell Fran what I'd done when I knew she wasn't going to blame me. I know. I still blame Sylvia.

Sylvia jiggles the bed a little, wanting me to say something more.

How can I be sure she's home to stay? I don't want to ask. I won't ask until I know she'll give me the answer I want to hear.

FORTY·ONE

When we can smell toast, Sylvia gets up and goes back out to sit with Fran. There is a long moment when I don't hear them talking. When Fran is not even telling Sylvia to sit down and eat. I know Fran is asking with a lift of her eyebrows, and Sylvia is shaking her head.

And then I hear Fran say in a low voice, "Never mind. Give her a little time."

Whatever Sylvia says is covered by the scrape of the chair she pulls away from the table. Fran's voice is clear, though, when it comes. "She's going to give you a second chance."

Sylvia asks, "How do you know?"

"She's been giving you a second chance all along. From the moment she didn't ask someone for help."

I hadn't thought of it that way, but Fran is right. Only now, when I have my second chance, I'm afraid to reach for it. I need to know Sylvia's here to stay.

I hear Fran say, "Tell me about that morning."

"I went food shopping," Sylvia says. "Walked around with this television picture of the three of us as a happy family. Like I didn't know Jim expected me to go with him. When I got back from the store, Jim was waiting here, and he was angry, so angry that he didn't find me here. I didn't want to lose him, I thought we'd talk things out when he settled down. The delivery boy brought everything in this big cardboard box, and I threw my clothes in it."

Fran says, "You got scared."

"I didn't want to leave," Sylvia says. "But I didn't want not to, either. I was crazy for a minute, for a few minutes, and then it was too late to turn back."

"So tell me the rest of it," Fran says, and I listen.

"Most of the first night, we drove," Sylvia says. "There was this bridge that went on for miles and miles. It was like a nightmare, the way that bridge went on."

"Bridges don't go on for miles and miles," Fran says.

"Twenty-five miles, I swear," Sylvia says.

Fran says, "Who could build a bridge for twenty-five miles?"

"Ma," Sylvia says in that tone she gets when Fran's making her wild.

"All right already, so after the bridge, then what?"

"We stopped in Virginia. I tried to call Casey, tell her I was coming home." Sylvia's talking fast, like she feels ashamed, too. Tears come to my eyes, angry tears. I hate Sylvia. But I'm also glad she's home.

"Then Jim was there, he cut the connection and grabbed me by the wrist, Ma, and twisted it. I was stunned that he got so rough. 'What's the matter with you?' I asked him.

"He never answered, just drove on. We stayed a couple of days in Atlanta, then headed north again. He told me we were heading for Canada. That's when I realized he was in some kind of trouble. When we stopped for gas in Pennsylvania, I locked myself in the ladies' room. He came around and banged on the door. I wouldn't go out."

Fran makes a *tsk, tsk, tsk* sound with her tongue.

Sylvia says, "I screamed at him to leave my stuff out there or I'd call the police. I'd say he kidnapped me."

"Oh, Sylvia," Fran says.

"My stuff hit the door," Sylvia is saying. "I didn't go out until much later, when someone wanted to use the ladies'."

"Why didn't you phone me?" Fran asks.

"I was too ashamed to call." Sylvia's voice changes, she's crying. "Ma, how could I get so mixed up?" I'm crying, too, pressing my face deep into my pillow so I won't make a sound.

FORTY·TWO

The first thing I hear in the morning is Sylvia's voice. When I went to sleep, my head was full of imagined fights, full of the mean things I could say when Sylvia tried again to tell me how sorry she is. This morning, I just listen. Sylvia is saying, "Her father would never forgive me."

"You're being too hard on yourself."

Sylvia makes some kind of huffing sound. "I can't believe this is my mother I'm talking to. Used to be if I only stayed out late on a date, you said you could never trust me again."

"You were a youngster then. I'm older now. Smarter."

"You're being very good to me, Ma."

"It's my job," Fran says, and I picture the way she shrugs.

Sylvia is right. My dad would never have forgiven her. Sylvia told me that herself when I was maybe six, before she married my dad. I had run away from her around then.

She'd taken me shopping with her. While she walked around racks and racks of clothing, I stared through the wide glass doors at the front of the store. I could see sunshine and people walking back and forth. Sylvia kept scraping hangers across the racks.

I didn't think about it. I just walked out.

When I got to the end of the block, I followed the side-walk around the corner. I wasn't allowed to cross the street by myself. I turned the corner every time I came to one, ending up in front of the store again. Because I didn't know what else to do, I went back inside.

About half a minute later Sylvia rushed past me, looking every which way. She was scared, like her whole world had caved in. I didn't call out to her, and she went on rushing around.

When she finally saw me, she cried, "Is this where you've been this whole time? I've looked everywhere for you, I thought I'd lost you." She swept me up in a perfumed hug, and it didn't matter that I had not been lost. I'd been found. Up to that point Sylvia had treated me like a doll too fragile to be played with. This time she smoothed my hair in a rough way and gave me a little shake.

"I'd feel terrible if I let anything happen to you. Your dad would never forgive me. Nothing happened to you, did it?"

I shook my head, nothing had happened.

Later, I'd asked, "If I was lost, would you be sad?" I like remembering that Sylvia said, "I would be very sad."

Sometimes I wonder if I just made it up so I could remember it that way. Right now it makes me feel like maybe I'm missing something. Maybe I should be in there having breakfast.

I pull on a sweatshirt over my T-shirt and hurry to the

bathroom. When I come out, Sylvia is saying, "I just need something to look forward to, Ma."

Fran replies, "Everyone does." She looks a little lost for a moment. She looks more like Sylvia's mother than ever before. "Everyone does," she says again as I slip into my seat at the table. There's a cinnamon doughnut and a glass of milk waiting for me.

When we do the dishes, Sylvia tells Fran she ought to get a dishwasher.

"It's just me now," Fran says. "I only use one plate."

"One plate three times a day," Sylvia says. "They do pots and pans now, Ma. You'd fill it up in no time."

Fran starts telling Sylvia about her friend Ina, who moved into an apartment no bigger than a closet. "She asked me, did I want to move into the empty one next to her," she says. "Can you see me in a little walk-up, three rooms and a cat?"

"You don't have a cat," Sylvia says.

"I'm getting one. You remember Mrs. Nolan, from the bagel store? Her cat had kittens, and by next week she'll be looking for homes for them. I've already claimed the marmalade."

"Marmalade?" I ask.

"An orange kitten," Fran explains. "I've always loved the idea of an orange cat sunning itself in the window where I'm doing my needlepoint."

"Ma." Sylvia looks like Fran's said something funny. "Needlepoint?"

"See how much you know? I've taken it up. I always meant to, but I could never sit still long enough. Now I'm old, I sit."

"Ma," Sylvia says, the way she sometimes does when she's annoyed with Fran. She doesn't look annoyed now.

No one mentions school. I don't have to pretend to be sick.

A few minutes later, the phone rings.

Fran picks up and says, "About time you called. I was getting worried." And then, "Is it a nice place?" And then, "Let me have your phone number." By then I'm standing next to her, and she hands the phone over.

"Paulie?"

"How are things there?" he says.

"Sylvia's back," I say without hesitation.

"Will you look at that, power of positive thinking," he says.

"What?"

"It's something I'm reading. Judy gave me a book," he says. "I'll call you again and tell you about it. I can't stay on right now, there's a little kid here. I promised him I'd walk him to nursery school. I just wanted you to know I'm fine. The people here are nice."

"I'm glad."

"Yeah, well, don't go thinking you're rid of me yet."

"I'll call you later."

As I sit down again, Sylvia's saying to Fran, "I just want to get the talk with the police out of the way first, okay?"

I ask, "Are you going to tell the police where he is?"

"I don't know where he is," Sylvia says. "I know where he said he was going, and that's what I'll tell them."

I get a panicky feeling. "Fran told them you were in Jersey."

"I know. I'll have to tell them the truth."

"All of it? Couldn't you get in trouble?"

"I'm not going to tell them anything that will keep me from coming right home." Sylvia gives me a weak smile. "I'll tell them I left you with my mother, okay? Everything should be all right."

F·ORTY·THREE

Fran wants me to help her do the grocery shopping, which so far means I pull the cart. I'm feeling very uneasy. I wish we had stayed in the apartment. But I know Fran wants to keep our minds off Sylvia.

Still, Fran is an unbelievably picky shopper. At the vegetable market, she sends somebody down to the basement storeroom to get onions because she doesn't like the ones on display.

At the bakery, she goes through the loaves of bread looking for the one with the most sesame seeds. Right over her head, there's a sign that reads PLEASE DON'T HANDLE THE BREAD.

At the butcher shop Fran wants to smell the inside of the chicken. The butcher lets her. Any other day it would be funny.

I ask her, "Why didn't we get a delivery?"

"I like to make my own choices," Fran says cheerfully. "In fact, I like to shop."

"Shouldn't one of us have gone with Sylvia?"

She gives me one of her sharp looks. "Do you mean 'gone with Sylvia' or 'kept an eye on Sylvia'?"

"I'm not sure." I'm reminded that Sylvia has always been

able to hear two voices. I think she must have learned this from her mother. "Maybe both."

"We have to let her know we trust her," Fran says.

"I guess." I won't feel better until we go home and find Sylvia there.

"I'm going to tell you what I told Sylvia this morning," Fran says in that no-nonsense tone of hers. "A good person is not the same thing as a perfect person. Good is good enough."

This isn't what I expect to hear.

Fran says, "Everybody has things to be ashamed of." She laughs a little. "If they don't, maybe they're living much too carefully. Not that I'm saying it was okay, what you did." She narrows her eyes at me as she says this last part.

"I don't know how to fix it," I tell her.

"There's almost always a way."

Which doesn't exactly give me any ideas. But what she says sticks to me.

As we're walking, Fran tells me she likes to go out to the movies on Friday nights. I say I like movies, even old movies.

She says she sometimes comes into the city to the museum on Saturdays. I say I like museums. Usually Sylvia's feet hurt too much to go there.

Fran says she has a few ladies over to play cards on Wednesday nights. I say I'm busy on school nights myself. I want to get good grades.

"A person could get used to Sylvia working nights, if they weren't alone in the house," Fran says. She glances at me as if to see how that went over. "Sylvia could date someone and it wouldn't have to be such a big deal. It could be fun, even."

I used to watch Sylvia get ready to go out for the evening with my dad. Sitting at her mirror, she looked like a movie star. Even the way Sylvia put on her lipstick was like a little movie. There was a time when Sylvia could be more fun. Was having more fun.

There was a time when it wasn't scary to be part of that.

Fran says, "I'm thinking Sylvia might not feel so desperate to get married if she had help with the responsibilities of raising a child."

"I'm not such a child anymore."

"That's what I'm counting on," Fran says as we walk home.

FORTY-FOUR

"We ought to go out more often," Fran says while we're waiting for the elevator.

"Why?"

"So you can get used to coming home and finding her there."

The elevator comes then and we ride up. "Paulie could come visit," Fran says.

"You mean it?"

"He looks like a person who likes cats, don't you think?" So I know she means it.

At the third floor, the door slides open and Razza steps in.

My heart races. I can only stare.

Razza winks at me. She gives me the creeps.

Fran's standing at the door so the elevator doesn't close, waiting for me to pull the cart through. She says, "Do you feel all right, Casey? You look flushed."

"I'm fine." I give the cart a yank to get it into position and roll it out. I feel shaky all over, sick to my stomach.

In the apartment, Sylvia's at the table, studying her patch of sky. She says, "The weather looks like it's clearing up."

I unpack the cart. I don't want to ask about Razza. I'd like to forget her. Maybe Sylvia feels the same way about how things went at the police station, so I don't ask.

Sylvia gets up to take the stuff for the fridge from me. It's the best and the worst moment we've had since she got back. In some way, giving celery and carrots to Sylvia is almost like I'm making a promise.

Maybe I want it to be a promise. I'm dying to feel like we're almost back to normal. It seems like we still have so far to go.

"I had a visitor while you were gone," Sylvia says when Fran comes in. She takes the chicken Fran bought and looks for her roasting pan. "A gypsy."

"A gypsy," Fran says. She's putting on water for a cup of joe. "You let her in?" And then, "I put the roaster in the oven."

Sylvia retrieves the pan, saying, "Ma, you always liked to get your cards read."

Fran asks, "Did she read your cards?"

"Well, no," Sylvia says. "We talked about some mystical book she's selling."

"The Mystic Pyramid?" Fran asks.

"You've heard of it?"

"As a matter of fact, I have," Fran says.

I'm taking my time digging things out of the bottom of the cart.

"So did she offer you any advice?" Fran asks.

"I don't want to go into all of it just now," Sylvia says. "The main thing she told me, act as if."

"Act as if what?" Fran asks.

"It's hard to explain," Sylvia says with a shrug.

I can't help smiling.

When Sylvia reaches over to ruffle my hair, it's a promise.

FORTY-FIVE

The old lady should be coming home soon. The money is in my book bag, the ring is in my pocket. Waiting for her at the subway station, I feel ready to see her. When I do, and when she sees me, the only thing I want to do is run.

Her eyes are fierce. "I brought this back," I tell her. I hold out the ring box.

The old lady's eyes seize on it so hard, it's like she already has her fingers wrapped around it. And then her eyes seize on me.

"Except for the money, that's all there is," I say. I'm shaking. "The other jewelry is gone." She takes the ring box and opens it. A little cry comes from her throat when she sees the ring inside. I tell her, "The money is here."

I'm pulling the bundle of money out of my book bag, holding it out to her. She shuts the box on the ring and puts it into the pocket of her coat. She accepts the bag with the money. She looks like she might cry.

"I wish I could get the other box back."

She doesn't say anything. It isn't enough, I should have known that. "Well, I have to go."

"Wait," she says.

If she yelled it, or looked at me in any way different than she does, I'd run. She holds me there with her eyes, eyes gone almost kind. I'm not sure it isn't worse.

"I won't ever do anything like that again." I hope I'm not going to cry. I hope we both won't.

She draws in a long quivering breath of her own. "My name is Martha Jane Clark," she says. She puts out her hand.

I don't know what she expects of me. Because I don't know what else to do, I shake her hand and say, "Casey Drummond."

"Surely not," Mrs. Clark says. "Casey. No. Are you named after your father?"

"No. After my grandmother."

Mrs. Clark raises her eyebrows and waits.

"Cassiopeia." I say it the way my dad used to say it, CAH-see-oh-PEE-yuh. "Cassiopeia Rose."

We both speak at the same time.

"Was it—"

"Did you—"

And stop.

"Was it your idea to rob me?" she wants to know.

"No." I'm glad she knows it wasn't my plan. Even though it doesn't change the fact that I did rob her.

"Do you live nearby?" she asks.

"No," I say, and then I can't keep myself from asking, "Did you call the police?"

"I was afraid to call the police," she says. There's no kindness in her eyes when she adds, "I'm old. I'm alone. I was afraid they would think I'd imagined the whole thing. It was one thing to say I was robbed, it seemed unreasonable to insist I was robbed by a child."

I remember Paulie said it was like that for most old people. I know a lot more now than I did before. I understand being all alone.

"Oh, it was a terrible thing you did," she says, and I can feel her anger. My skin goes hot. I thought I could face this, now I'm not so sure.

"I'm sorry I took the money. I'm sorry I took all the money, even. I didn't need so much, I was too scared to think."

"I didn't care about the money," she says. "I took it out of the bank months ago. The jewelry, too. It belonged to my sister. She's in a nursing home. She went in to recuperate from a broken hip. She never was able to convince herself there was a good reason to come back out. She's healthy. Strong, even."

"You were going to give it to her?"

"I thought if I showed her the jewelry, it would remind her. Bring her closer to the memory of better days."

Like the way I kept buying Ring Dings right after Sylvia left and eating them, even though they didn't taste nearly so good to me as they used to. It's like a reminder of better times, even if it can never be quite the same, it's better than nothing.

"The money was different. I wanted her to come out of there, to come with me on a little trip." She presses her hand to her mouth for a moment. "I hoped she'd never want to go back."

"You showed the ring to her?" I hate to think she hadn't shown her sister the jewelry. "All those months ago when you took it out of the bank, you showed it to her?"

"I did. She only wanted to wear it. She wouldn't leave that place."

"So, what happened?"

"Well, I told her it was all stolen. I told her a masked man broke into the apartment. And now she's coming home. She's coming to live with me."

"Because you got robbed?"

"Yes." A little half smile breaks out and her eyes twinkle. For a moment she looks almost young. Looks like Sylvia, somehow. "She said I always needed to have someone looking out for me, even as a girl."

"You mean she thinks you can't take care of yourself?"

"I mean exactly that. And I'm going to go on letting her think so," she says.

"Mrs. Clark—" I make myself look into her eyes. "Mrs. Clark, I'm sorry. I'm just . . . sorry."

FORTY·SIX

We talk a little more. She wants to know that things are all right for me now. That I won't have to do that again. We walk together a little ways. I hate that she's trying to be so nice. That she's so brave.

At the corner I tell her I have to go a different way. I can hardly wait to get away from her. When I look back a couple of minutes later, I can't see her. I start to run.

And run. I run until my breath is coming fast and hard. I run until my side hurts.

Still, I run until that pain is all I can think about. When I can't run anymore, I stop, look around. I'm in a part of the neighborhood where I've never been before. I'm not lost. And if I don't feel like a really good person, I'm maybe good enough, I don't have to hide from anyone anymore.

I notice it's going to get dark soon, I really should be going home. Fran and Sylvia will worry. I turn a corner, walking so the stitch will go away. I'm hot, I unzip my coat. After a few minutes I realize it's warm out. I don't need a jacket at all. Funny I didn't notice earlier.

Sylvia is waiting for me outside the building. She wants to go see the parakeets. On the way, she says, "Ma thinks you're going to give me a second chance because I'm your mother. I think you'll do it because there isn't anybody else."

Right away my eyes burn with held-back tears. She almost sounds angry, but it's like Sylvia just opened a window to let me see how bad she feels. How unloved she feels.

Only I can change that.

"You're stronger than I am, we both know that," she says. "Maybe it's because you lost your mother when you were so little. You know how to handle sadness. When I lost your dad and mine so close together, it was the first time I lost someone, Casey."

I hadn't really thought of it that way. Hadn't looked at it as Sylvia having two sad things happen to her while I had only the one. I felt bad about Sylvia's dad, of course, but I didn't miss him the way she must've.

"I felt terrible, leaning on you so hard for support. That's why I wanted another man in my life."

"It's okay."

"You must've thought I was acting like your dad would be easy to replace."

"No. I just didn't like your boyfriends." I remember my talk with Paulie. When he asked me how I would feel about Jim moving in with us. "Well. I didn't want anyone to take my dad's place, either."

"No one could take his place, Casey. I told you that."

"They might. You took my mom's place."

Sylvia is silent for a moment. Then says, "That's the nicest thing anyone has ever said to me."

I throw my arms around Sylvia even though we're still walking. "I'm glad you came back."

"Me, too." And she hugs me around the shoulders, we walk like that, clinging to each other. It's awkward, but it makes us feel better. "It was like I got lost for a little while, Casey. I never meant to hurt you."

"Does that mean you'll stay?"

Her voice is fierce when she says, "It means you will never get rid of me."

We've arrived at the parakeets' window. Because the weather is warm, the curtains are open. We can see only the occasional tips of wings and tails. Water splashing. They're playing around in a pan on the bottom of the cage. And then one of them climbs up the side of the cage to a perch, feathers ruffled and damp. This parakeet is such a pale chartreuse, it's nearly yellow. "The bluebird of happiness," Sylvia says.

I grin at the bird as it shivers its feathers back into place. It looks down at us and natters in a friendly way. "Yes, she is."

"How can you tell it's a female?" Sylvia asks.

"It's just a feeling."

FORTY·SEVEN

Fran forgot to salt the roast chicken. We keep passing the shaker back and forth. They're having one of their usual friendly arguments. Sylvia's telling Fran she ought to paint the kitchen if she's putting in a dishwasher. "Maybe you'd think about painting the cabinets," Sylvia says.

"Paint good wood?"

"The wood finish is pretty beat-up looking."

"It's an old house," Fran says.

"That's why it needs paint."

"The whole place needs a good paint job," Fran agrees. Sylvia opens her mouth to argue, then shuts it.

Fran adds, "Everything looks gray to me lately."

Sylvia's answer doesn't come so quickly this time. When it does, she says, "It's all those white walls, Ma. They aren't good for the heart. For the soul."

"I think you may be right," Fran says. "When you pay somebody to come in and paint, white is all they want to know from. Slap! Dash! That's the kind of job they can only do with white paint. So if they don't do a good job, it won't show."

"You used to like white walls, Ma."

"When I liked white walls, I didn't need a hint to remember where I am." She looks around her. "Walls like you have, they're like a map. Pink walls—oh, this must be the living room."

Sylvia laughs out loud. "Okay, Ma, you've gone too far."

I love the way Sylvia laughs.

"I'm exaggerating," Fran says. "I admit it. But that house is too big for me alone."

The look on Sylvia's face is hard to read. Fran offers her a little more encouragement, saying, "I wouldn't mind a yellow dining room like you have."

"Ma," Sylvia begins, and it doesn't sound like she's going to go for it. Fran puts a hand up to stop her.

"I know it's a cliché, moving in with your old mother. I was ashamed to ask. Now I see we can do for *each other*," Fran says.

I say, "We're moving in with you?" Like it's a big surprise.

When I look to see what Sylvia thinks, she's looking at me like we're in the desert and I'm holding the last glass of water. I nod, the way she does when she gives an okay.

"You don't really want a yellow dining room," she says to Fran.

Fran flips her hand at Sylvia. "Such a stubborn. Even hospitals don't paint white these days. They found it out scientifically, color is better."

"Yellow would be nice in the dining room," Sylvia says,

and for a moment, I see the old sparkle in her eyes. "With that blue-and-white willow-pattern china from Casey's mom."

"I like my own china," Fran says.

Sylvia shakes her head.

Fran says, "We could display the china. On Grandma Capotosto's hutch. How's that?"

"Just say yes," I say.

Sylvia says, "We'll always have these different ideas, Ma. All of us."

"It won't be easy," Fran agrees.

"Say yes," I tell Sylvia, knowing she will.